Adventures of Pachelot

Book #2

Fort Brokenheart

By

Wendy Caszatt-Allen

Mackinac Island Press

for the love of reading

J CAS

Fort Brokenheart is the second exciting book in Wendy Caszatt-Allen's series, 'The Adventures of Pachelot.' You will not only fall in love with Pachelot (*Pash-uh-low*)—an Australian Shepherd who can communicate with certain humans, you will also fall in love with her storytelling, as she takes you back to a time of fur traders, sailors, Native Americans, and 100% adventure.

First Edition

Library of Congress Cataloging-in-Publication Data on file

Adventures of Pachelot #2: Fort Brokenheart

Summary: Pachelot journeys into the wilderness on a quest to discover the
fate of his Algonquin friend, Keta, with Badger, Keta's younger sister, traveling
through the perils of the Empty Lands.

This book is a work of fiction. Names, characters, places, and events are works of
the author's imagination or are used fictitiously. Any similarities to any person is
coincidental.

ISBN 978-1-934133-09-5

Fiction
10 9 8 7 6 5 4 3 2 1

Cover Illustration by Angela Taratuta

Printed and bound in the United States
A Mackinac Island Press, Inc. publication
Traverse City, Michigan

www.mackinacislandpress.com

For Shawn,

Love and Adventure always ⟿

Fort

Brokenheart

Chapters

Chapters

Prologue

The struggle between the French and the British for the beaver trade in Old Northwest results in one of the deadliest wars ever known on the North American continent: The Beaver Wars. As allies of the British, the Iroquois plunder and attack Algonquin tribes allied with the French and relentlessly drive them out of the beaver-rich wilderness territories. These abandoned areas of wilderness become known as The Empty Lands.

When the Illinois Indians treacherously murder a Seneca chief during a meeting at Fort Mackinac, the Iroquois take to the warpath in revenge. Their target is La Salle's newly constructed fort on the Illinois River. Deeply feeling the loss of his ship the Griffon, LaSalle has named his new fort Crevecoeur, which means Broken Heart. But the Iroquois are seeking revenge and in the process they will try to destroy a French fort that is becoming a center for the French beaver trade.

Now Pachelot must journey into the deep wilderness on a quest to discover the fate of his Algonquin friend, Keta, lost when La Salle's ship, the Griffon, sank in the angry waters of Lake Michigan. Badger, Keta's younger sister, travels with Pachelot, guiding him through the perils of the Empty Lands.

The dangers of the Beaver Wars are all around them. But one danger in particular, a hidden, deadly danger disguised as a gift, will prove to have the destructive power to wipe out entire Indian nations. Those tribes unlucky enough to come in contact with it, will be unable to survive the encounter.

I

The Beaver People

"Quiet now, Pachelot!" Badger warned as we carefully crept forward to the edge of the woods. "We don't want to be seen."

"Don't worry," I growled softly, stepping delicately behind her.

Of course, no one can be as quiet in the woods as I can and by that I mean, being a dog, I have certain advantages that humans do not. And so it was a bit of a surprise when I sort of stepped on a hidden stick, which broke like a brittle bone with a crack as loud as a gunshot.

We froze.

We waited, hearts pounding, but the woods around us remained empty of threat. No alarm was raised.

Badger leaned close to my ear and whispered. "We've got to stay quiet. The Amikwa should be very close. If Keta is their prisoner, we don't want to get caught too."

Keta.

We had been looking for Keta ever since the sinking of La Salle's ship, the *Griffon*. For a minute it seemed as though the bright autumn light dimmed around me as I remembered those last frantic moments, caught in the grip of the wild lake storm, when I watched my friend Keta disappear into the dark waves.

Guiltily I bellied down into the drift of leaf mold close to where Badger crouched under the low branches of a pine and put all my senses on full alert. We were looking for the Amikwa, the Beaver

People. If we found them, we would find Keta.

We hoped.

Cautiously, I peered through the screening brush. Suddenly Badger tensed and, drawing in her breath with a sharp gasp, she elbowed me in the ribs.

"Pachelot! Look!" she hissed.

I *was* looking. Through the screen of trees we peeked out onto a maze of waterways twisting snakelike through tall reeds and around the brushy bumps of beaver lodges.

"It's beaver, Pachelot!"

All around the quiet pools of water I could see the stumpy brown creatures. Some were idling on top of their lodges, combing their sleek brown fur, others were moving slowly on the bank. Their musky scent seemed to fill my nose. A shiver, like a late fall breeze, passed over me and my tail quivered with excitement.

"They don't know we are here," Badger whispered excitedly.

But that wasn't all. On the far bank of the beaver pond, looking quiet and peaceful in the bright afternoon light, was a small Indian village surrounded by a log palisade.

"The Amikwa?" I barked softly.

"Has to be!" Badger's answer was fierce as she narrowed her blue eyes, squinting against the slanting rays of the sun. "This is the last village before the Empty Lands, Pachelot. That village has to belong to the Beaver People. It all fits my medicine dream!"

As a young shaman of her tribe, Badger often had powerful medicine dreams. When her brother, and my friend, Keta, had disappeared, Badger began having dreams about Keta's Manitou, the beaver. Through the dreams she became convinced that Keta had somehow survived the sinking of the ship and that we would find him with the Beaver People. Probably, she had told me, he was a prisoner; otherwise he would have found his way home before now.

"Let's go then," I wiggled with impatience. "Let's break in and find out if Keta is there!"

"We have to be patient," Badger said quietly. "Patient and brave and, above all, alert. Danger is all around us."

I wuffed and sat up a little straighter in the concealing shadow of our hiding place. Of course danger was all around us! And it would be up to me, Pachelot the Brave, to watch out for it.

I don't mean to brag, but after we rescued Keta, who knows what praises would be sung about me around the voyageur's evening fires? Perhaps I would compose a song myself...

My petite canoe,
through wind and snow,
is paddled by Mighty Pachelot!"

I think it was the music that inspired my great idea. I leaned close to Badger. "I was just thinking," I growled softly. "Maybe we could disguise ourselves, you know, like a couple of deer, and then sneak right into their village."

Badger turned and her blue eyes sort of rolled, as if I might have leaf mold for brains.

"Wonderful idea," she replied. "But, Pachelot, what kind of animals do you think the Amikwa hunt and eat?"

I thumped my tail thoughtfully. "Ah, I believe that might be deer?"

I began scratching myself, mostly in embarrassment, but also because I thought I might have a flea hanging out somewhere on my left shoulder. Suddenly Badger grabbed me and pulled me close.

I saw immediately what had startled her.

A small group of Indian boys in breechcloths and moccasins had burst through a gate in the palisade and were running up the riverbank.

"Is Keta with them?" Badger asked anxiously.

I narrowed my eyes and sniffed the wind in concentration, but none of those boys seemed to me to be Keta.

Whooping and yelling they charged up and down, waving clubs and hitting a wood-filled ball back and forth to each other. I could see at once that they were experts at knocking the ball away from each other and, I should know, being somewhat of an expert myself in chasing round things that roll.

It was exciting as I watched one boy, in a daring move, snag the ball away from the very foot of his opponent. This brilliant maneuver was met with wild calls and laughter and I almost forgot myself and barked out loud. But I swallowed the bark and turned it into sort of a sneeze at the last second.

Badger gave me a brief worried glance. "You're not getting sick, are you?" she asked.

"Of course not," I wuffed indignantly.

She ruffled my ears.

The beaver had remained unconcerned and paid no attention to the new activity of the ball-chasing boys.

Beaver are rather dull, stumpy creatures,

I thought, restraining myself with a huge effort. How they could ignore such excitement and not join the boys in their chasing was beyond my understanding.

It wasn't until the ball came sailing over to plop in the water that the beaver showed any concern. Without alarm, they slid smoothly into the water. Their small brown faces peeked out of the rippled surface as the boys tumbled into pond after the ball. Splashing water high in the air, shouting and wrestling with each other, the ball was finally retrieved and the laughing, yelling squabble of boys retreated to the bank.

"Keta is not one of those boys," I growled this information to Badger, but I think she already knew it.

As the pond quieted again, the beaver lumbered back to the roofs of their gnarled homes, spinning water from their fur with quick shakes.

"Do you think anyone would notice if I just sort of joined in the game?" I quietly wuffed in excitement.

Badger swiftly clamped her hand over my muzzle. "Hush! Those boys are very close. They might investigate a barking dog." Her dark braids swung in annoyance as she shook her head in warning at me. "This has to be the Amikwa, Pachelot," she continued in an excited whisper. "See how honored the beaver are? They are allowed to live here quietly and no one bothers them."

"So what's the plan?" I mumbled into Badger's palm.

She removed her hand. "We have to wait and watch. If Keta is a prisoner in that village, we need to know it before we can safely make a move."

She was right, of course. So we waited and watched for what seemed like a whole dog lifetime. On the faint breeze I could smell the twists of smoke that rose from the domed houses behind the palisade and floated into the darkening air. The moon rose, looking like a large pale version of the ball the boys continued to chase. The shadow of the timber crept across the ponds and a cricket bravely jumped over my paw.

I nipped at it and earned a scowl from Badger.

It was high time we did something adventurous, I thought. I was just going to point this out to Badger when, suddenly, I was distracted as a whiskered nose broke gently through the surface of the pond just a few feet away from where we hid. Spreading a lance of ripples, it moved across the water. I watched, barely able to sit still, as other plump, sleek forms began to move about along the edges of the ponds.

All around us the beaver were coming out to do their evening work.

"Badger?" I whined with the agony of restraint.

"Be still, Pachelot." She was completely unsympathetic. "If they think we are trees, maybe they will come closer to us."

Yes, great, I thought. Beaver within biting

distance and I had to be a tree—very difficult for a dog, I can tell you.

Off to my left soft sounds of shaking were punctuated by the slow noisy fall of a sapling. "It's for food," Badger whispered next to me. "They will sink those small trees below the deepest ice of the frozen time. It's the winter food of the beaver."

Not as good as a nice bone, I thought.

Badger's eyes were round with the wonder of being so close to the work of the animals. "They're all around us," she whispered in delight as the dark shapes moved forward to work again.

"I could go bite one for you," I offered.

"I've never been this close to Brother Beaver," she said ignoring my suggestion.

One old beaver tugging a sapling behind him paused for a moment on the rim of the bank. Something wasn't right. Catching the warning from his sudden watchful stillness, I froze concentrating on what he had sensed.

Somewhere nearby a twig snapped. Almost

immediately I smelled the danger—*men!*

But before either the old beaver, or myself, could do anything about it, the quiet of the evening was ripped apart by an exploding burst of light.

The old beaver was knocked back as the roar of the blast slammed across the ponds.

Violent slaps of beaver tails crashed on the water in warning.

"Keep down!" Badger whispered urgently.

No problem there. Someone had a musket, and I in no way wanted to be mistaken for one of the beavers now frantically diving into the water and disappearing below the surface.

In seconds they had vanished leaving behind the still form of the old beaver.

Even as the echoes of the shot faded, cries of alarm had erupted from the village. Indians carrying bows and arrows and war clubs leaped through the splashes of fading light heading for the pond. The Indian boys, their ball clubs swinging over their heads, joined them.

Then, silent as the distant stars pinpricking the new darkness overhead, two men stepped out of the dusk of the timber to stand silhouetted on the shadowy bank.

The Hideout

We watched the Indians surround the men. Deadly arrows were nocked to bows and heavy war clubs were raised menacingly in the air.

"We have to get into that village!" whispered Badger.

"Should we slip in now?" I growled low in my throat.

"No," Badger decided as she watched the men carefully surrender their muskets. "The Indians look upset. They would be sure to see us if we tried to walk across that open ground to their village."

The warriors began to escort the men under careful guard toward the village. Two other Amikwa retrieved the body of the dead beaver. They did not look at all happy.

We will have to wait until things settle, I thought. If the Indians were mad enough about the beaver they might turn their anger on any strangers found in the area.

"We'll go into the village in the morning," Badger decided. "It might be dangerous, but we have to find out about Keta."

"Right," I thumped my tail.

"For now, let's get back to the canoe. Follow me, Pachelot, as quietly as you can!"

Silent as a falling leaf, Badger slowly retreated into the shadows of the woods. Staying low, I followed her.

As we put distance between the Indian village and ourselves, we began to move faster.

Soon we came to the small backwater of the larger river where we had hidden the canoe.

"Quickly, Pachelot," said Badger anxiously scanning the dark woods. "Let's get out of sight."

All around us night rose in the woods. The trees were only dark shapes harboring the secret rustle of animals that love the night.

It did not appear that we had been followed.

Badger ducked and squirmed her way into the hidden hut-like structure she had constructed earlier. I was close behind her.

Badger was very clever when it came to hiding in the woods. This time she had used her canoe tilted on its side and leaning into the uprooted overhang of a large cedar as one wall of the hut. She had then piled and arranged branches and brush over the canoe and the overhang to create this hiding place. The gentle gurgle of water, a quick escape route if necessary, was only a few feet away.

"We are in beaver country," Badger had said.

"So let's take a lesson from them and have a water escape route handy."

Inside our hiding place Badger arranged a blanket and some furs as a bed. Badger's canoe was slightly smaller than a full size canoe, but still there was plenty of room for the two of us to huddle together.

"No fire tonight, Pachelot," Badger murmured. "We don't want to risk someone finding us. That village will be extra alert now that those strangers have walked in."

"Who do you think they are?" I had not been able to get a good scent of them, and then gunpowder had laced the air making it almost impossible to smell anything else.

Badger shrugged, rummaging in a pack for some food. "I don't know who they are, but my guess is they are fur trappers."

She brought out a pouch of dried corn and some strips of dried venison for me. I gobbled those down almost before they left her hand.

"Will they be in trouble from the village for shooting that beaver?" I sniffed hopefully around my paws trying to find an overlooked tidbit of meat. No luck.

Badger crunched on her corn. "Maybe," she said thoughtfully.

Badger is such a slow eater, and by that I mean in the time it took her to slowly munch her handful of dried corn I could have eaten a whole herd of deer. Listening to her munch and crunch in the dark beside me I suddenly longed for a bit of old dried bone to gnaw on.

First chance I get, I promised myself, I would have to find one someplace.

Finally, Badger was finished. She settled down on the ground pulling the furs and blanket around her. I hunkered down in the crook of her knees with my chin resting on her ankles. The night might turn frosty, but we would be warm enough.

"I think what we need is a bold plan, Pachelot," said Badger, her voice muffled by the blankets.

"Oh, yes," I thumped my tail. "I certainly agree with that. A plan that calls for a disguise, and maybe pirates."

"I agree about the disguise," said Badger. "I'm a little doubtful about the pirates."

"I suppose so," I scratched my ear in annoyance. "Maybe pirates would be hard to find out here where we are."

And where we were, remember, happened to be just at the edge of the Empty Land. That's what Badger's people called it. It was empty because the Iroquois enemy, trying to get the beaver trade for the English, had driven out all the tribes allied with the French that had been living here. It was too dangerous a place to live in now. The village we had found today was probably the last one for many wilderness miles. So that meant that even pirates would not be around.

"Good. Then it's settled," Badger yawned.

"Okay," I agreed.

There was a silence as Badger sighed and snuggled deeper into her blankets. Clearly, she was intending to go to sleep.

"Hey!" I gave her ankles an impatient thump with my front paw. "What exactly is settled?"

"Hush, Pachelot. I'm tired." She yawned again.

"I'll start howling if you don't tell me exactly what you are planning," I threatened.

I couldn't be sure, but I thought maybe she stifled a giggle. "Your howling saved my life once and so I wouldn't mind a bit," she said, referring to the time Keta and I had saved her from a hostile Indian attack by pretending to be monsters called Big Heads.

I nipped at her toes that were just peeking out from under the blanket.

"Okay!" She swatted at me and the canoe rocked, threatening to collapse on top of us. We lay still holding our breath, waiting to see if our hideout was going to collapse on our heads.

A small pinecone sifted through the brush-top ceiling and hit me on the end of my nose. I sneezed.

"Oops," said Badger.

Nothing happened.

"Seriously, Pachelot," said Badger when it appeared that our hideout would not fall in on us after all. "I haven't got it all worked out yet, but I think the thing to do is to just walk into that village tomorrow and see what we can find out."

"Just walk in." I was doubtful.

"And see what we can find out," she said. "If Keta is a prisoner then we can discover that."

"The trick being not to become prisoners ourselves," I pointed out.

"Well, yes," Badger agreed. "That would not be part of the plan. I think you are right and we will need some sort of disguise."

"But probably not deer."

"No," she laughed. "Probably not that."

I rested my chin on my paws and gave a tired

wuff. "I suppose I could always bite somebody if they get rowdy with us."

"Goodnight, Pachelot," said Badger as she mumbled into sleep.

An Old Enemy

The crows woke us in the early dawn. The woods around us were filled with their big black bodies as they flapped from tree to tree, sounding their harsh notes. The trees surrounding our hideout were crimson with the touch of the frosty night.

We crawled out from under the canoe into the crisp morning air spicy with the smell of nuts and dead leaves. I did some minor racing around, stretching out the muscle kinks of the night and splashing in the cold water while Badger carefully repaired the slight damage to our hideout, making sure it was invisible once more.

High overhead a squirrel chattered irritably at me, flicking its tail in annoyance as I danced under his tree. I gave a sharp bark in his direction and watched, laughing, as he whisked around the tree trunk spiraling into the higher branches. It was clear that he didn't want to take any chances in case it turned out that I could climb trees.

I can't, of course, but squirrels are not the most intelligent of animals. I grinned wickedly.

Badger laughed. "Come here, you Terror of the Woods. I have something for you."

Giving the squirrel one last bark, I bounded over to Badger, spraying her with a bit of leafy ground as I careened around her. I couldn't help it really. Morning air sometimes hits me that way.

"Settle down, O Terror of the Woods," Badger said laughing and trying to grab hold of me. "We have serious work to do today."

So I plopped down beside her, panting happily, while she knelt to tie something into the red scarf that I wear around my neck. I sniffed at it suspiciously. It turned out to be two crow feathers.

"What's that for?" I was worried in case the feathers ruined my nice scarf, which had been a gift from Sieur de La Salle himself.

"Look, Pachelot," said Badger and she stood up in front of me.

I looked at her and noticed that she had done a few things to herself as well. She had fastened some shells and feathers into her long black braids. The feathers were blue and reflected the color of her strange eyes, emphasizing them. She had changed into a white deerskin dress with tiny red beads worked into the fringes, but continued to wear her hide leggings for warmth. She wore her regular moccasins, but had decorated the tops with more short strands of shells. Over her shoulder she had slung a pouch made of muskrat and decorated with fancy quills dyed many colors. I thought that Badger had probably done that herself as I had seen her work with quills many times before.

"We are dressed up," I realized, growling in approval. "Is this our disguise?"

"Yes," said Badger. "I am a young medicine apprentice and I am going to say I'm on a medicine quest. You will be my medicine dog. With your own badger's eye, I think you will be convincing."

And by that Badger meant that, because I have one blue eye and one brown eye, I would be very distinguished.

We had had this discussion before so I said nothing about it now. Badger's people believe that blue eyes are a sign of the badger who is the keeper of stories. Badger herself has blue eyes and so is considered by her people to be a keeper of stories, a sort of shaman. I have been considered a storyteller too, on occasion, but I always claim that my blue eye is my pirate's eye and that it makes me look fierce and dangerous. I remember La Salle's lieutenant and my friend, Iron Hand Tonti, once commenting on my possession of those qualities.

I don't want to brag.

"I think that this village will respect us in these roles," said Badger. "With luck, they will allow us in to rest. Then we can see if Keta is there."

"I hope so," I gruffed. Squirrels were one thing, but Indians with war clubs were something else again.

The sun was well up when we reached the Indian village. This time we made no attempt to hide, but walked boldly in the open.

The village scouts saw us almost at once. My ears twitched as I caught the sharp signal whistles they gave. But no one rushed out with war clubs.

Just inside the palisades of the entrance we were met by an ancient Indian woman so bent and wrinkled she looked like the weathered sides of an old tree. In her clawed hands she carried a brown bundle wrapped neatly with a slender grass twine.

My nose twitched as I identified what she carried as beaver. I also detected the fact that the skin was wrapped around beaver bones.

Hmmmm...bones. I think maybe I drooled a bit as I lolled my tongue trying to look as though I wasn't thinking of a way to snatch that bundle from the frail old hands that held it.

But I am, above all, a refined sort of dog and so I buried the temptation like I would have buried the bone itself.

Badger held out her hands in a gesture of peace. The old woman squinted up at her from her brown and pinched face and smiled a welcome.

"Good day," said Badger. "I am Badger. I have been wandering on a medicine quest. I saw the smoke from your village. May we be allowed to take shelter here for a few hours?"

"I am Alsoomse," said the woman, her voice cracked and as whispery as dry leaves. "Our scouts have seen you approaching and recognized your medicine. You are welcome here."

"I see you are about to tribute Brother Beaver," said Badger. "May I be allowed to assist?"

The woman nodded her head in agreement.

Badger and I accompanied the woman at a very slow hobble out of the village and down to the edge of the beaver pond. The water was smooth and unruffled in the calm of the day. There were no beaver in sight.

Badger selected several fist-sized rocks for the woman who then carefully bound them up inside the hide. I watched keenly looking for a chance, in case one should be offered, to get at the bones I knew were in there.

Would I be able to quickly snag one away when no one was looking?

The woman and Badger carefully lowered the stone-weighted bundle into the water. The old woman briefly sang a cracked and wailing song. Then they gently released the bundle into the water.

Sadly, I watched as it sank out of sight. While

I can find almost anything on or in the ground, water was a different matter altogether. I wuffled unhappily.

The woman lowered herself to the ground to catch her breath. Badger settled beside her.

"So the beaver is your dodem?" Badger asked. A dodem was the spirit of a respected animal. Clans considered their dodem to be their ancestors.

"It is," said Alsoomse. "Yesterday strangers came to our village and an evil one killed one of the elders with an iron stick that roared fire. The elder had to be honored, his body returned, so that his enemies cannot disturb it and so his people know that we still respect them."

I realized she was talking about the beaver. This was a ritual that Alsoomse's people would do whenever a beaver was destroyed. I knew that a clan did not kill their dodem for food.

"Now," said Alsoomse struggling to her feet. "Come with me to my wigwam. You may rest and perhaps we may tell each other some stories."

We followed the slow crooked walk of Alsoomse back to the village. As we entered, a group of young warriors were leaving for a morning hunt. They carried spears and bows and arrows. At their heels ran a group of ragged dogs, which barked and growled at me as they sped by.

I ignored them.

Rabble.

Alsoomse's village was a very busy place. Everywhere people were working. Some women were drying meat hung on stick frames over low burning fires. Others stirred birch bark containers of the afternoon soup. Elderly men sat in doorways smoking pipes or sharpening stone tools. A group of children ran past carrying armfuls of dried reeds, which they gave to a circle of women who were weaving mats.

There was no sign of the two strangers.

There was no sign of Keta. It could be that Keta wasn't even still alive. But I quickly drove that thought out of my mind. Badger felt certain he was alive. We just had to keep looking.

"Here, here," Alsoomse gestured us into her wigwam which rested somewhere in the middle of the small village.

Badger and I ducked inside. The dim interior smelled like smoke and meat and people and—cat?

And not just any cat! Curled up on a blanket near the fire was a mound of shaggy, snarled fur out of which two yellow eyes opened in an evil glare. As it saw me, the creature leaped to its feet hissing and spitting, fur on end.

"Archeveque!" I barked.

IV

The Big Chase

Surprised, Badger made a lunge to try and hold me back, but she was too late. Sailing over the fire and landing in a tangle of blankets and baskets, I sprang for that flea-infested clot of fur.

I missed completely.

"Pachelot, no!" Badger tried desperately to warn me, but I didn't even hear her.

With a yowl of rage Archeveque bolted out of the wigwam.

Barking like the Hound of Doom, I was after

him.

Archeveque, the enemy I thought I would never see again, streaked through the village like a small yellow tornado. I surged right behind barking and snapping at his tail whenever I thought it might be in reach.

"Where's Keta?" I barked in wild fury.

"Like I'm going to stop and discuss it with you, drool face," Archeveque spat and whirled around through a small forest of frames drying meat in the sun.

We plowed through the piles of dried reeds, scattering them like ribbons in a hurricane. Children shrieked and women yelled flailing at us with the whippy ends of the reeds as we swirled away.

"Is he still alive?" I yowled in frustration, snapping my teeth inches from his scruffy cat hide.

"If I knew I would tell you!" Archeveque raced to the top of a framework of poles from which hung a variety of breechcloths and blankets airing in the morning breezes. The frame wobbled under his weight.

"Come down, you bag of fleas," I barked at him.

"You're too fat to catch me, bone breath," he hissed down.

"I'll show you who's fat!" I growled and leaped straight at him.

My teeth snapped air. Moving like water through sand, the yellow devil melted away and was no longer clinging to his unsteady perch as I went crashing into the frame. I heard him laugh as the frame collapsed under me and I went down in a tangle of clothing.

"Watch out, fish brain," I barked struggling free, or almost free because a pair of breechcloths had tangled around my head, and now I was wearing them, sort of like a cape. "I'm not finished with you yet."

In a yellow streak the cat was off and I was

after him.

A woman stirring her birch bark container of soup over a fire shook her spoon at us. Archeveque ran light-footed around her. I swerved and managed to knock into the container sending hot soup to douse the flames of her fire with a hiss and snap of sparks that sounded like the cat I would soon chomp into pieces when I caught him.

We managed to skirt another larger container of water set over a fire that was, apparently, just beginning to get warm. The woman attending it had a large stick she used to swat at Archeveque as he stormed past. She missed him but managed to clobber the woman behind her who was trying to rescue her pots of shelled peas.

The cat stormed around for another tight pass around the stick wielding woman and her container. I made the quick, brilliant decision that I could cut him off if I leaped straight across the container of water.

Not so brilliant as it turned out.

I'm sure it would have worked if my breechcloth cape had not snagged on the nearby pole supporting the water. It pulled me up short just like a rope around my neck and, yanking me out of the air, deposited me in the pot of water.

Archeveque laughed and the woman beat on my head with a wooden spoon.

"You probably needed a bath anyway," Archeveque taunted.

I scrambled free upsetting the pot in the process and leaving the woman and her fire drenched in water.

Archeveque clawed his way up the side of a frame where a woman sat weaving and snagged the fibers of her work as I chased him off, leaving a torn tangle of threads in his wake. The wet breechcloth cape flapped heavily about me as I followed, threatening to tangle in my feet, but it did not slow me down.

Someone threw a spear at us, which just missed me by inches and buried itself into the side of a wigwam as we steamed pass. The two warriors standing outside the entrance, armed with spear and war clubs, yelled but did not pursue us.

Were they guarding that wigwam?

But I had no time to think about that because now the village dogs, those the hunters had left behind, had joined me in the chase. They boiled up behind me, a snarling, yipping mass of teeth and tails. I really don't think they even understood what was going on. They were in it for pure enjoyment of the chase.

Truthfully, they did more damage then I did. They didn't seem to care where they charged. Some even went through wigwams and burst out the other side. One group barged into what must have been the council hut and emerged covered with ceremonial feathers and playing tug of war with a wampum belt.

Many people began chasing them to reclaim these items. The ball-playing boys of the evening before appeared on the scene and added a lot of whooping and hollering. Things like pots and war clubs were flying through the air.

"Stop, you yellow devil," I barked at the streaking creature just out of reach of my iron teeth.

"Catch me, stick chaser," he sneered and suddenly leaped onto the roof of a low wigwam. Thinking I could make that jump too, I hurtled myself into the air in a monster leap, the wet breechcloth cape floundering around my shoulders.

And fell short.

And crashed into the side of the wigwam.

Which began a slow and dreadful sway.

"Now look what you did, your gracefulness," observed Archeveque as the whole structure began a slow collapse to the ground.

V

Prisoner

Using his iron-like claws, Archeveque scaled the wooden stakes of the palisade and disappeared over the top as I was surrounded by warriors pointing long sharp spears at me.

I was so tangled in the breechcloth that I couldn't run, or fight, or really do anything useful at all. So I bared my teeth and growled. At least the Terror of the Woods would die with a snarl on his face!

But just then Badger pushed her way past

the circle of warriors and threw her arms around my neck.

"Don't hurt him!" she cried. "He is my medicine dog."

Fortunately, the circle of spear pointing warriors listened to Badger. They saw her blues eyes and my pirate's eye and realized that maybe they should not act hastily. There are potentially disastrous results from killing medicine animals, you know.

The warriors lowered their spears. Three or four of the men nodded to each other as they agreed upon some unspoken thought. One of them gestured and several warriors grabbed Badger while others threw a rope around my neck.

I snarled and barked and tried to free myself with the result that more Indians threw a net over me. The thing about nets is that the more you struggle, the more entangled you become, but the more tangled and trapped you get, the more you panic and the more you struggle. You begin to see,

I'm sure.

"Don't struggle, Pachelot," said Badger. "It's okay."

That was easy for her to say. She was only being hoisted onto her tippy-toes by two unsmiling braves with their braided hair flopping in their faces.

So I stopped struggling, but I did not stop growling. It wouldn't hurt for these warriors to maintain a little respect for us.

They dragged us over to the wigwam guarded by the two warriors with spears and war clubs. Alsoomse stood at the doorway.

"Don't worry," she told Badger in her thin old voice. "I will speak to the council. We live in a time of danger. Everyone is nervous."

You're telling me, I thought as rough hands dragged me along.

"Thank you," said Badger, and we were both shoved inside the very dark wigwam. Some sort of blanket was slapped down over the opening making the darkness almost complete.

I lay engulfed in netting, sniffing the close and dank air, as Badger quickly worked me free.

We were not alone.

"We're not alone," I wuffed to Badger.

"Hello?" said Badger. "Is someone there?"

"Of course someone is here," answered an irritated sounding voice from a dark corner of the wigwam. "You don't think they would have warriors with war clubs guarding an empty wigwam, do you?"

I think that perhaps both Badger and I had hoped it would be Keta. I had not scented Keta when we were shoved inside, but the voice from the dark was definitely not Keta. The hope died hard into bitter disappointment.

I growled.

"And keep that Terror of yours on a leash if you have one," said the voice turning urgent. "I won't hurt you, but I am myself injured and could not fight off an attack from that furry fury of yours."

I assume he meant myself, the Terror of the Woods.

"It's okay," said Badger. "He will behave himself—won't you, Pachelot?"

And by that she meant that I had caused enough trouble for one day. But I am sure that you can see how it had not been my fault at all.

"So are you the ones responsible for all the delightful village panic?" the voiced asked pleasantly.

It was a man hidden in the darkness of the wigwam and he didn't really smell too dangerous.

Still, you never knew.

I growled again just to make sure he understood about the Terror of the Woods reputation.

"Hey! Easy there—I said delightful!" He was obviously getting the message.

"Just a minute," said Badger. I could hear her rustling in her bag. In a minute there was a small *snick* and a tiny flame flared into being. It grew quickly and steadily and I could see that Badger was holding a small clamshell bowl containing a happy blue flame that danced on its surface.

Badger had used this shell bowl before. All I knew about it was that it held some sort of oil that would burn for quite a long time.

Badger held up her light and now we could see a puddle of shadow that was a man slumped against the far wall of the wigwam. His long legs were stretched out in front of him and his bare, very dirty feet stuck straight in the air.

"I see now," he said, and his voice was a bit strained with a sudden emotion. "You are the angel of light."

As Badger moved closer with her small light, we could see the man better. He was dressed in buckskin and smelled like tobacco and muskrat. But that last scent may have been coming from the scruffy muskrat hat that lay crumpled on the floor next to him. His bare head was a mess of tangled hair clotted with dirt and blood. The little flame dimly lit his thin bearded face. He had a large crooked nose. His dark eyes watched us alertly, but now we could see that he was also in some pain.

"Quickly, Pachelot," said Badger kneeling beside him. "He's hurt."

"I'm okay," said the man and he tried to brush her away. But Badger would not be brushed. She leaned forward to get a better look at his injury just as the man leaned forward to push her back. Their heads met with a firm *clunk* that sounded like a small war club bruising a large unripe pumpkin.

"OW!" Badger cried, clutching her forehead, and the tiny flame bowl wobbled as she almost dropped it.

The man himself said a few choice words, but they were muffled as he slumped back into the wall from the force of their collision. To be fair, he wasn't in as good a shape as Badger, having been a prisoner and all. Still, it seems as though a tough man could have taken a knock on the head better than that. And then he was sort of flapping his hand at her as she bent over him again, like he was waving.

"Stop that!" Badger commanded. "You are injured and I can help."

"Well, I certainly am injured now," the man said. "I think I'm seeing stars."

"Don't be such an infant," Badger scolded. "Hold still and let me look at you."

"You better let her," I growled. "She'll do it anyway."

The man looked nervously in my direction. "Did he say I would be good to eat?"

Badger laughed, her scowl disappearing like an elusive scent on the breeze. "No. He was just encouraging you to be still while I look at your injury." She carefully set her small bowl of light on the dirt floor beside her. "I know how to handle injuries. So, let me look. Please."

"Fine," the man sighed. "I suppose allowing a girl with a man-eating dog to look at my injury is the least of my worries."

The man-eating dog grinned widely showing his wicked white teeth. And by that I mean I just panted a little with attitude.

"Thank you," said Badger as the man lay back, apparently done with head bashing and hand waving. "My name is Badger and this is Pachelot."

"My name is Nicholas Robair and you have blue eyes," said the man in sudden wonder, catching the light of Badger's eyes as she bent nearer him.

"Where are you injured?" asked Badger impatiently.

"Besides the lump you just gave me on my head, it's really just my arm that is hurt."

Badger ripped away a length of blood-soaked sleeve to reveal a long and ugly gash high on the outside of his arm.

"Hatchet wound," said Robair briefly. "Inflicted by my friend."

But by the way he said the word friend, it

was apparent he didn't mean friend.

"Here, Pachelot. I have need of your—um—cape, is it?" Badger gestured.

"Be my guest," I growled, not at all displeased at having the sodden mess of breechcloth untangled from around my neck.

Badger took the wet cloth and, using a portion of it, carefully wiped away the dried blood. From her pouch she produced various sweet smelling dried leaves and things and crushed them together into a sort of paste mixed with a lard-like compound, which she warmed over her small shell-bowl flame. She smeared this mess on the wound and then bound it with the remaining portion of breechcloth.

"Thanks," said the man. "Ah. That feels better. Apparently you do know what you are doing."

"I said so, didn't I?" Badger carefully returned her supplies to her bag.

Robair carefully flexed his thin arm. His

fingers were long and his hand looked strong.

"So was your friend the man who killed the beaver?" asked Badger.

"Yes. That was thoughtful of him, wasn't it? His name is Charles Segan. He managed to convince the Amikwa that I had done the deed. They weren't too happy about that."

"They weren't too happy with us either," I barked a contributing comment.

"Are you sure your dog isn't thinking about tasting—say, my right arm or one of my legs?" Robair edged away from me.

"Pachelot?" Badger giggled. "He is very fierce, of course."

"Fierce is my middle name," I agreed with a vigorous tail thump.

"I believe that. He sounded like a whole tribe of hostile Indians running through the village," said Robair. "I thought it was a massacre in progress. What was he doing?"

"Chasing a cat," said Badger, giving me

a look.

"A cat?" Robair threw back his head and laughed loudly.

The blanket flap was whisked aside and two warrior heads peered at us. Badger quickly doused her flame and Robair stifled his laugh. After a moment of suspicious, shadowy glaring, the warriors withdrew and the blanket flopped back into place.

"Call him a cat if you want to," I growled. "But we all know what that ratty ball of fleas really is."

"Hush, Pachelot," Badger ruffled my ears and then she kissed me on the nose. So much for the man-eating reputation.

Robair laughed again, only softly this time. "It sounds just like you two are really talking to each other."

I growled my disgust and Badger giggled as she re-lit the bowl of small fire. Really, I decided, a future powerful shaman should learn a more dignified emotional expression than giggling. Who would take her seriously? *Please allow me to save your life with my medicines—giggle, giggle.* I ask you.

Robair started to sit up but Badger pushed him back to the ground. "Wait," she said. "Rest and get your strength back. Here." She handed him a cake of pemmican that she also had in her pouch. "Is there any water in here?"

"No," said Robair, hungrily chomping into the food. He was like a big bear ravenous after a winter sleep. "They haven't given me anything to eat or drink since they threw me in here last night."

"Well, that isn't right," said Badger, suddenly angry now. She got to her feet and marched to the door.

"Badger," I barked anxiously going after her. "Are you sure you know what you are doing?"

She didn't answer me but stepped up and tossed aside the blanket covering. We were instantly looking at the business ends of two spears that were pointed menacingly at her throat and my head.

VI

The Escape

Badger stood straight and glared at the young warriors who threatened us. I added my best deep in the throat growl that no one had ever failed to interpret as: *I'll tear you to pieces if you do something stupid.*

"What is it?" It was Alsoomse hobbling rapidly toward us. She was carrying a covered basket and a birch bark pail of water, which slopped gently over the sides as she hurried up.

"This man in here is injured," said Badger.

"He needs food and water."

"I'm sorry I can't help that man," said Alsoomse. "He is the one who killed our elder and he must be punished. We are only waiting for the return of the main hunting party before we decide what should happen to him. He cannot be your concern."

"Anyone who suffers is my concern," said Badger.

Alsoomse looked at Badger's fierce blue eyes and could not doubt the truth of that statement.

"I'm sorry," she said again and her old face was even more wrinkly with worry lines. "Here is some food and water for you and your demon."

Demon? Now I was a demon?

"Thank you," said Badger accepting the basket and bucket. "What will happen to us?"

"We will have to decide that as well," said Alsoomse. "If the hunt has been good perhaps the destruction your demon caused will not be important."

As she turned to hobble away I could see people busy picking up the mess that our chase had caused. It didn't look good for the demon.

Back inside the wigwam, Badger gave us all water with the majority of it going to Robair, who drank thirstily, splashing a dribble of it in his beard. I protested a little about him getting so much of the water and wasting a good portion of it on his chin. After all, I had just had quite an active morning, being a demon and all, and I was thirsty. Badger was unsympathetic and it was obvious that Robair did not understand a single word I said.

"You smell like rotted potatoes," I told him, watching him wipe driplets from his scruffy, crooked-nosed face.

"Nice dog," he replied, and sort of smiled at me.

"We are looking for my brother, Keta," Badger told him. "Do you know if there are any other prisoners being kept in the village?"

"There are no other prisoners," said Robair.

"Just me and a bunch of sorry spiders who spin their webs in the roof of this blasted wigwam. What happened to your brother?"

So Badger told him a little bit about the sinking of the *Griffon* and how we thought that Keta must still be alive somewhere.

"I kept dreaming about Keta's Manitou," said Badger. "That's why we came here to look."

"I see," said Robair. "Your brother's spirit guide is a beaver then."

"Yes," said Badger softly, watching the tiny flicker of light in her shell bowl. "But I will tell you this. Keta's Manitou isn't just any beaver."

"How is that?"

"When my brother went on his vision quest a few years ago, he had a difficult time connecting to any spirit animal. He fasted for days, deep in the wilderness, waiting for the vision that would serve as his Manitou. When it finally came to him it was more powerful than he could ever have imagined.

"Keta's Manitou is the giant White Beaver

Manitou himself."

"I have heard of him," said Robair seriously. "Sometimes in tales around the fire a voyager will speak of it. The White Beaver is a Manitou of legendary power and purpose."

"Yes," Badger agreed. "That was why it had taken Keta so long to find his vision."

"So you sought out the Amikwa, the beaver people," said Robair. "That seems logical."

"But he isn't here," said Badger, disappointment heavy in her voice.

"But that disease of walking fur was," I reminded her. "He didn't survive that shipwreck if Keta didn't."

"That's true," Badger agreed.

"What is?" asked Robair.

"We have to keep looking," said Badger. "That cat that my man-eating terror was chasing earlier was also a survivor of the sinking of the *Griffon.*"

The man-eating terror let his tongue hang

out in a happy pant.

Robair looked nervously in my direction. "Well, I guess we both have things to do. You need to keep searching for your brother and I need to find that fine friend of mine, Charles Segan, who not only saw to it I ended up in here as potential sacrifice material, but also took off with my musket, my canoe, and all the furs I had gathered. How is a man supposed to get rich if his buddies keep stealing his stuff?"

Badger and I looked at each other. No clue, really.

"So," continued Robair, "now that you've helped me and I'm feeling better, we'll have to break out of here."

"Certainly," said Badger. "It shouldn't be too hard."

"Not too hard?" He sort of snorted a laugh and his tone of voice said plainly he thought that Badger was completely crazy. "It's insanity, my blue-eyed friend! We will have to get by two angry warrior-guards carrying spears and war clubs..."

"I can handle the guards," Badger interrupted confidently.

"I'm sure a small girl with a ferocious dog will be more than a match for trained warriors," said Robair, clearly not believing a word of it. "But then we must make our way through an entire village that is wall-to-wall kids, dogs, women, more trained warriors, and old men..."

"That's where I come in!" I barked enthusiastically. "I know all sorts of ways to get through stuff like that."

Robair raised an eyebrow at me. "I don't know what that dog just said—if anything—but I know that he can't climb a ten foot wall with spikes on top..."

"There's always the front gate," Badger murmured.

"And then, of course, there is the small matter of staying hidden long enough to escape out of this territory before the warriors, searching every nook and cranny for us, find us."

"Yes," agreed Badger unruffled. "I think that what you have said would just about do it."

"About do it!? It should about do us in!"

"Don't exaggerate," said Badger. She rummaged around in her bag and took out a small packet that smelled spicy with the scent of mint.

"What's that?" I barked.

"Sleep leaves," she said. "I have a plan."

"So, say we manage to escape." An exasperated Robair was still trying to argue, although I don't know why he bothered. It never does any good to argue with Badger. "And then into what? We are on the edge of the Empty Lands, in case you didn't know. There is nothing beyond here but miles of forsaken wilderness patrolled by wandering bands of hostile Indians looking for scalps."

"Well, your scalp won't provide them with much," I muttered considering the muddy mat that he was wearing for hair.

"See? The dog agrees with me," he said.

Oh, brother.

"Pachelot, see if you can get that nose of yours into the breeze outside the door. Be careful!" Badger reached for the remaining water and crumpled the sleep leaves carefully into it. "I want to know what you smell out there."

"Careful is my middle name," I muttered as I quietly settled myself low near the flap of the door. It wasn't difficult to poke my nose past the fold of the blanket covering.

At first all I could smell was a beavery warrior smell. That wasn't too surprising as one of the warriors was sitting on the ground leaning against the side of the wigwam just beside the door. Cautiously, I put all my concentration into my nose and, as usual, discovered a whole bunch of things.

The fires had been rebuilt and the soups were again cooking. The meats had been re-hung and a muffled odor of drying venison tickled into my nose. The smell of the Amikwa were everywhere in varying intensities. And then, suddenly, there was something else mixed in with all the smells of the village. It was just a shimmer of something and I almost missed it. I stayed very still, focused, inhaled quietly.

My nose quivered.

Yes. There it was again.

No mistake.

Silently I withdrew into the wigwam.

"Well?" Badger demanded.

"You aren't actually talking to that dog, are you?" asked Robair.

"Yes, she is actually talking to me, mud head," I barked and had the satisfaction of watching him start back, unsure if the man-eating Terror was going to attack him or not.

"Pachelot! Be polite!" Badger scolded.

"Did that—that—*dog*, just insult me?" Robair tried to struggle to his feet, but Badger held him down.

"It isn't important," she said, succeeding in

calming him.

Ah, well. Badger had a soft spot for a lot of low creatures. For her sake, then, I would try. But seriously...

I added a little evil grinning in the direction of Robair just for effect.

"Stop it, both of you!" Badger had had enough. "We have serious business at hand here. Pachelot, what did you smell?"

So I told her. "Rain!" I barked.

"Yes! That's what I thought," Badger was excited. "So it will be easy. We'll just wait for it and then we will make our move."

"Wait for what?" Robair wanted to know.

"The rain," Badger explained. "Pachelot smelled rain. We'll wait for it to start raining and then we will make our move."

"Right," Robair sighed, apparently knowing at last that Badger would be getting her way. "Then I suppose that before I sacrifice myself to the madness of this plan, I have time for a little nap." And he rolled over with his back to us and in a few minutes began to make noises that sounded like wind in pain.

I think he was snoring.

The rain came just after nightfall. And there was a lot of it.

Alsoomse had brought food and drink to the warriors guarding our wigwam. In the sudden downpour of rain, the warriors set their cups of hot soup down just inside the wigwam door out of the weather while they scurried about bundling up in blankets and skins as protection against the cold and wet. At that moment, Badger was able to slip into their soup the sleep leaves and they never knew it.

The darker it got, the heavier the rain began falling, driving everyone else in the village into their cozy wigwams for the night. The guards outside sat on the ground leaning on either side of the doorway, trying for as much protection against the weather as they could.

And that was where the sleep leaves finally overtook them.

Soon, even Robair could hear their snores rumbling into the night mixing with the drumming of the rain on the roof and the rush of wind tearing the leaves from the trees.

"Now is our chance," said Badger. "I'll go first. We will meet at the gate."

"We won't be able to open that gate," Robair protested. "Why don't we just nip behind this wigwam and climb over the palisade. I'll help you over."

I looked at him with great pity. "Dogs can't climb," I reminded him with a gentle wuff.

"Oh, I forgot," he said. Now, I don't believe that all of a sudden he could understand me. I think it was just a matter of realizing the truth of the situation. Even a turnip head like his could get it.

"We should be able to find a small space

somewhere around the gate that Pachelot can squeeze through," said Badger. "Then you and I can climb the palisade."

"Okay," agreed Robair. "But let's not put everybody at risk. You go ahead and climb over. I'll take the dog to the gate and help him through."

Badger hesitated to agree. I was a bit doubtful too. Would Robair be able to do as he said? Could we trust him?

Finally, Badger nodded her head. "That's our plan then. We can meet back at my canoe. Pachelot can show you how to get there."

I thumped my tail in agreement. Robair gathered up his muskrat cap, which was all he had, and we were ready.

Cautiously, Badger pulled aside the blanket covering the door. A pitch-dark maelstrom of heavy rain swept in.

"Perfect," grinned Robair. "Let's go!"

VII

A Good Hiding Place

As we stepped outside into the blackness of the night, we were engulfed by the rain and wind. It was a cold, late fall rain, the kind that cleans the trees of leaves and makes way for the winter snows. It was only an instant and we were all drenched.

Robair helped Badger to find the palisade wall only a few yards behind the wigwam and boosted her up.

"Can you make it?" he shouted softly up at her in the downpour of the rain.

"Yes I can!" Badger wasted no time and began scaling the wall like a cat.

After being sure that she was going to be able to make it to the top, Robair turned back to me.

"Okay, Pachelot," he entwined his hand in my scarf. "Use that nose of yours and get us to the gate."

"Right!" I wagged my sopping tail enthusiastically spearing drops of water sideways behind me.

I started off around the corner of the wigwam, but we didn't get far when suddenly Robair stopped me.

"Wait a minute," he said. "I need shoes."

What could I do? I needed him to open the gate for me. He needed me to help him find the gate. I couldn't just leave him. So, I stood there anxiously in the pouring, roaring rain while he carefully extracted the moccasins from one of the sleeping guards and put them on his own feet.

"Okay, let's go!" I growled.

But apparently he wasn't finished. Robair nipped back inside the wigwam and emerged with the net that had so recently imprisoned me.

For an instant, I thought he had in mind to bind me again and leave me in the village. I began backing away. But that wasn't his plan. Carefully, as though he were holding the thinnest gossamer of spider web, Robair delicately draped the net over the sleeping guards, thoroughly entangling them in the mesh.

"There," he said, satisfaction in his tone. "That should just about do it."

And then he backed up and tripped over the outstretched foot of the guard whose moccasins he had just stolen.

Nicholas Robair went down fast and hard and landed on the sleeping form of the other guard.

That's all it took.

Both guards were instantly awake and would have had us recaptured in a blink if they hadn't been tangled in the net. There was a lot of yelling and whooping and thrashing about, but Robair had again wrapped his hand in my scarf and was yelling at me to get to the gate.

We thumped and floundered along. I made the best speed I could hampered by the stumbling man attached to my neck. Dragging Robair was worse than my breechcloth cape. Flapping along in a stooped over stumble, Robair managed to stay on his big feet as we made it to the gate and the whole village came alive around us. The rain began to ease up.

Frantically we searched around the gate looking for an opening large enough for me to squeeze through. I tried to dig around the edge of the bottom tossing a fountain of mud in the air, most of which spattered on Robair.

"Thanks a lot!" he grunted as he exerted all his strength in pulling at the edge of the door.

At last I was able to just wiggle through.

I barked a warning at Robair, but he had already given a jump and was quickly scaling the wall. It was too dark for the Amikwa to see him, but the village dogs knew right away what we were up to and sent up the alarm.

Robair dropped to the ground next to me just as the Amikwa began to work to open their gate.

"Hurry, Pachelot!" Robair urged, his hand again grasping my scarf. He was completely blind in that black night.

I began to lead us toward the woods, but behind us the gates suddenly opened enough to allow the village dogs to boil out in pursuit. It wasn't long before they were all around us, a snapping, yipping surging wave of wet dogs.

"I'm not happy about this!" Robair shouted.

But these were village hunting dogs and they loved to run more than anything else. For them this wasn't so much a chase as it was a chance to run, barking loudly, and in a wrestling mob. The danger lay in that they would alert the warriors to where we were.

"I have a plan!" I barked and veered toward

the beaver ponds.

Robair, of course, had no idea where we were going and so it was a complete surprise to him when I suddenly dragged him into the water. He immediately let go of my scarf.

"Pachelot!!" he exclaimed. "What are you doing? Are you trying to drown me?"

Now the rain had almost completely stopped and the wild wind was dying out. Behind us the warriors of the village, carrying blazing torches, were heading toward the barking of the village dogs. Dogs which, by the way, love to chase and run, but really don't like to swim all that much.

Robair, looking over his shoulder saw it all and understood that we were going to get caught. He didn't know what to do about it.

I did.

Using all my strength and weight, I leaped at him and knocked him back into the water. He fell sending up a big fountain of water into the faces of the barking dogs. While he struggled and fought the deepening water to regain his feet, I caught his shirt in my powerful teeth and began to drag him toward the nearest beaver lodge.

After their sudden bath of pond water, the village dogs stayed on the bank barking and whining, disappointed that we were giving up the run in favor of going swimming. I wasn't sorry to disappoint them.

Robair struggled and sputtered like water on a hot stone but, to give him credit, it didn't take him long to understand what I had in mind.

"Okay! Okay!" He shouted at me spitting and sputtering in the water. "I understand—*splaw, cough*—what to do! Let me go, please, before you—*splutter*—drown me!!"

As I could see that that was a real possibility, I released him. Together we quickly swam to the beaver lodge.

When we got to it we discovered that it was an old lodge. There seemed to be a lot of debris knocking untidily around its edges. It would be perfect.

"This is perfect!" said Robair, finding me in the cold water next to him. He was shivering as he placed his hand on my back for guidance. "We'll have to go under, you know. I hope you're up to it. I hope *I'm* up to it," he added, wrapping his arm securely around me.

Taking a deep breath he plunged under the water and took me with him. It was a scary thing to do. We couldn't see anything and we were not exactly sure where the opening to the beaver's tunnel was. Together we swam down, Robair groping with his free hand in front of us.

I had to rely on him. I can't smell underwater.

It turned out that because the lodge was an old one and had been abandoned for newer constructions, the tunnel had long ago fallen apart. It was easy for us to break into what was left of the hidden shelter inside the lodge.

Beavers build their lodges like low domed-shaped houses and they can contain several compartments. Some lodges have a dripping-off place and then higher compartments for warmth and dryness, as well as areas to store food.

Robair and I emerged into a cramped compartment that was almost roomy enough for us to get completely out of the water. Robair, who seemed to be as long as a boat pole, was forced to recline with his legs still resting in the cold pond. I was able to shake water from my fur and, being more flexible than my companion, I was able to curl into a ball on muddy, but not pooling wet, ground. I tried to crowd as close to Robair as I could to share warmth. The man was shaking so hard I thought maybe he would shake the lodge apart around us.

We had adequate ventilation through the sticks and probably enough mud had crumbled away in this old structure that, had it been broad daylight, we would have been spotted. But beavers are excellent architects and the old bones of the trees piled high around us gave us some protection from the night and the coldness of wind and diminishing rain.

"For a dog, you sure have your share of brains," said Robair, ruffling his hand through my coat. His shivering was subsiding a little.

"And for a human who can't understand a word I say, you sure know how to follow a lead," I told him.

He laughed. "I haven't a clue what you are trying to say, but I can imagine."

Outside we could hear the dogs barking and the Amikwa shouting to each other. I sure hoped that Badger had made it to the woods okay and was well hidden.

We waited for what seemed like hours until the rain began to pick up again and the Amikwa, apparently deciding that warmth and dryness were more important than hunting us, gave up the search and returned to their village.

We waited some more just to be sure.

"Well," sighed Robair at last. "As much as I hate to get into that water again, I think that now would be the time for the rest of our escape."

I thumped my tail in agreement.

Robair, once again, got a firm grip on me and together we plunged back into the icy cold pond and emerged seconds later sputtering and spitting and paddling our way to the bank.

We came out of the water on the opposite side of the village. The rain was a steady curtain of water on our heads as we emerged and warmer than the icy grip of the pond. It did not cheer us.

I guided Robair into the woods where we enjoyed some protection from the rain, but not a lot as the wind had driven most of the leaves from the trees. We stumbled through the wet undergrowth, going slower than normal because Robair, cold and still not recovered from his first injury, was having difficulty moving very fast. Eventually, I led us back to the hidden shelter that Badger had built for us.

It was the beginning of dawn as we emerged into the clearing and the world around us pearled into sight. It was no longer raining. The graying woods dripped uneven rhythms of residue raindrops and the distant call of crows echoed in the stillness of the dawn woods.

"I hope you know where you are taking us," Robair gasped. He was still stumbling along, but it wouldn't be long now before he would be unable to keep on.

"It's okay. We're here!" I barked.

And we were.

But something was different.

I twisted free of Robair and ran to the far side of the overturned tree that had hidden Badger's canoe shelter.

Both shelter and canoe were gone.

VIII

A Demon Drops
From the Sky

"Badger! Badger!" I barked frantically into the early morning stillness surrounding us. Behind me Robair slowly collapsed to the ground like a bag emptying of air.

"Pachelot!"

And then I saw her hurrying toward us. She had appeared from somewhere, but just at that moment I didn't care from where. She was no longer dressed in white but had changed back to the browns that hid her so well in the woods. I hurtled myself at her and gave her face a good sloppy licking. She should know better than to worry me like that.

"Stop it, Pachelot!" She laughed and gasped for breath as she tried to hold my wiggleness. "Come on. We've got to help Robair."

And that was true. Robair looked like a half-drowned muskrat as he lay sprawled on the ground. He was soaking wet and very muddy. Leaves had stuck onto him making him look bushy. He was shaking with cold, but he had a big grin on his face.

"When I make my fortune," he said as Badger tried to help him to his feet. "I'll make arrangements to run through late October rainstorms for my health. Ah, life is good!"

And then he collapsed again and this time seemed to go unconscious.

Badger, of course, knew what to do.

She disappeared into a strange pile of

driftwood that rested near the bank of the river. When she reappeared she was carrying an assortment of blankets and robes and her pouch.

"How did you find all that in that pile of sticks?" I barked and padded over to check it out.

"It's not a pile of sticks. It's the canoe in disguise," she said.

And it was. She had somehow arranged a pile of small trees and sticks over the canoe so it looked just like a mound of brush snagged at the water's edge. The canoe was tied securely to the low branch of a nearby tree, but I could see that it was ready for an instant launch into the currents of the river in case escape became a sudden necessity.

"Clever!" I barked approval.

Meanwhile, Badger had been busy with Robair. She had gotten him out of his wet clothes and wrapped warmly in the blankets and robes. His shivering had almost stopped. She was carefully lighting a very small fire in a deep depression she had dug in the ground. Over this carefully controlled flame she was heating something in a small bowl.

"Stay alert, Pachelot," she warned. "Keep that nose to the breeze and let me know if you smell anybody coming after us."

So I did. But there was nothing except squirrel, crows, wet leaves, pine, and maybe a small trace of brother porcupine.

Finally Robair woke up enough to drink the liquid Badger had prepared for him.

"Thanks," he said. "I'll be okay now. I'll start on in a little bit. I'll try and catch up to Segan. Sometime I will. He won't like it when I do."

"It's okay," said Badger. "We're going in the same direction. You can come with us."

"How do you know we're going in the same direction?" Robair and I asked the question together.

Robair gave me a look. "What's he barking at?"

"Alsoomse told me the direction your friend

took from the village," said Badger.

"He's not really my friend you know," said Robair.

"He went into the Empty Lands," said Badger. "That's where my brother is."

"How do you know that?" Robair hitched the blankets closer around himself. His crooked nose was red. He sniffed.

"I just do," Badger told him. "You can come with us. There's room in my canoe and going by water will be faster. You can catch up to Segan easier."

Robair squinted at the paling sky. Feathers of clouds scudded high in the blue. The sun was brightening, but the day was not warming up.

"Okay then," he decided. "Where is the canoe?"

"Good!" Badger smiled.

"Are you sure about this?" I wuffed.

There were several difficulties with this arrangement as I saw it. First, Robair was a big man and Badger's canoe was a small birch bark canoe. Cozy for a dog and a girl, but add a giant man with long legs into the mix and trouble logically follows.

After much maneuvering and the invention of clever words of distress, Robair managed to get himself under the driftwood disguise and into the canoe. He had to half-recline and his long legs extended almost the entire length of the little birch craft. He covered himself warmly with blankets and furs. After wringing as much water from them as she could, Badger spread his wet shirt and trousers over the top of it all to try and dry them in the air. Robair insisted on wearing his muskrat cap on his head, even though it was still a bit damp.

"I like it there," he said. "The only thing I would like better would be my pipe."

Then, Badger knelt in the bow and was easily hidden.

That left me to find a spot in the middle somewhere, half on Robair's bony, muskratty smelling knees and the few bundles of Badger's supplies.

When we cast off from the bank, the little canoe rode low in the water. Any sudden shifting of weight could cause us to scoop in water and sink like a stone. Because we were in disguise as a large snarl of brush and river debris, we could not paddle. We had to allow the current of the river to drift us along, slowly and uninterestingly, as we traveled in the direction we had to go.

And the thing about that direction was that it had to take us right past the village of the Amikwa.

It was late afternoon by the time we got underway. Robair had managed to get a paddle into the water, hidden among the overhang of the branches disguising us, and even though he could not paddle, we had some steerage. It would not have been a good thing if we had drifted right into the bank below the village.

As we approached the village the beaver smells from the nearby ponds wafted over me, but I lay as still as I could. We stayed close to the far bank where there was also an overhang of branches to further protect us from someone realizing what we really were as we drifted along on the smooth current of the narrow river.

Everything was going well. Robair had managed to stifle his sniffing. Badger crouched like a statue. I, myself, had turned to stone.

No one paid any attention to us as we began to drift by the village. A few Amikwa working in the corn stalks outside the palisade looked up from their work and glanced in our direction, but no one was interested in a clump of brush slowly spiraling down the river.

And then disaster struck.

Suddenly, something seemed to drop from the sky to land heavily on top of us.

Something that yowled like a demon as it fell from the sky.

IX

Warpath

The yowling creature on top of our floating disguise had a long tail, scrawny and yellow, that dangled through the branch roof only inches from my nose.

Archeveque!

My teeth snapped of their own accord.

I promise I didn't think about it at all.

Robair clobbered me with his foot.

"Don't bite him!" he hissed, and the canoe rocked crazily with water slopping over the side.

"Quiet! Be careful!" warned Badger. But we had seen the danger and both of us froze as the canoe wobbled disastrously and threatened to sink under us.

Clumps of driftwood nobody cares about. But a clump of driftwood wobbling along like a half drowning thing and being ridden by a yowling cat is very interesting indeed. Several Indians began to leave harvesting to come down to the river's edge for a better look.

And then there were the dogs. Dogs who had lately had the privilege of chasing the yowling cat.

They clustered along the riverbank in a yapping, snarling, eagerly bouncing, tail-wagging mob. They made false plunges into the river, spraying water and snapping at each other. The Amikwa began yelling at the dogs and trying to get them apart. This was not an easy thing.

Our canoe stabilized. We continued to drift past the now very alert and active village. Archeveque raised his voice and yowled and *marowled* even more vigorously.

"This is crazy!" Robair snapped. Before anyone knew what he was doing, he grabbed that sinister tail that was lashing the air inches from my nose and gave it a quick yank.

Thunk! Archeveque crashed through our bushy roof in a shower of dead leaves and broken branches and landed eye to eye with me.

"Don't eat him, Pachelot," Robair said urgently.

As if I would. Anything that ate that mothball would get sick and die. Instead I showed him my teeth—pretty much all of them.

Archeveque was clearly terrified. His eyes were so wide they were only dark holes in his head. His fur stood on end in great spiky clumps. His ears were laid back and he hissed like something leaking a lot of air.

"Easy now," Robair muttered, and then he did something that I found truly amazing and incredibly brave, especially for a man with a crooked nose who smelled like muskrat.

In one easy motion, Robair threw his still slightly wet shirt over Archeveque bundling him up completely. Then he scooped the cat up in his arms and had that monster clutched and cuddled to his chest where he began a steady stream of low murmuring to the squirming bundle he held. It was, in my opinion, a quick way to die. If that treacherous feline got loose, Robair would be facing a throat-ripping menace.

The other amazing thing was we didn't tip over. Robair had moved so quickly and smoothly that the canoe rocked gently but did not take on water.

"Quickly," he said to Badger. "Throw something overboard where they can't see from shore. Make sure it splashes. We want them to think the cat jumped or fell into the water."

Badger looked about for something to toss overboard. We couldn't throw out supplies. What could we throw? At my paws lay part of one of the branches broken off by Archeveque's entrance. I picked it up and Badger took it. She tossed it into the water so that it splashed.

Hopefully no one would now be interested in a catless brush pile floating downstream.

Soon we were past the village. We continued to float. No one came after us. The barking dogs and the cries from the village began to fade with distance.

Had we been that lucky?

Carefully, Robair peeled back some of the shirt so Archeveque could push his face out. Robair stroked that evil head with a vigorous kneading motion, which caused Archeveque to close his eyes and—PURR?!

"There now," said Robair as he patted and petted the creature. "You're safe now, you old pirate. You were very brave. Very, very brave."

This did not look good.

"Are you going to toss him over and drown him now?" I barked.

"Pachelot!" Badger and her soft spot again. She was peering carefully between the branches. "No one is following us. I think it worked."

Carefully, Robair let all of Archeveque out of the shirt. The cat planted himself on Robair's chest hooking long talon-like claws in and out of the blanket in a crazy thread pulling rhythm. Robair laughed and the canoe wobbled.

"Just what do you think you are doing?" I growled.

Archeveque waved his tail in insult at me, but did not break the rhythm of his kneading paws. "Look, bonebrain, I like this human. He gave me fish once. And I am not going to stay in the wilderness alone."

"Pachelot," Badger called gently from the bow of the canoe. "Ask him what happened to Keta."

"Tell her I don't know," said Archeveque curling around and settling himself in a ball tucked under Robair's chin. "I think he's around here somewhere."

And he closed his eyes.

We continued to drift down the river. Sometime late in the day we pulled into the riverbank to rearrange some things. Badger scooped out the water sloshing in the bottom of the boat. Robair got dressed again in his mostly dry, but very wrinkled clothes. Archeveque stuck to him like a burr. And by that I mean, he was mostly on Robair's shoulder clamped tightly to his shirt.

We had a meal of dried corn and pemmican. Robair begged some dried fish from Badger and fed bits of it to the cat. Archeveque took each piece as though he wasn't thinking about ripping off Robair's fingers as he did.

"You old pirate," said Robair laughing and did that petting thing that made Archeveque close his eyes and purr—a purr that sounded like rusty knives carving rock.

"I need some exploring time," I told Badger.

"Go ahead. We'll take these branches off the canoe. We can travel faster without them. Don't go too far."

"Right," I barked and bounded away into the woods very happy to be leaving maniac cat and man far behind.

I found rabbit scent right away and happily followed the zigzag trail of it under fallen trees and through the underbrush. I knew I wouldn't catch any of them, but it was fun to follow their trail.

Suddenly, the woods opened into a small clearing. The ground was deep golden grasses and, at the edge of the clearing, I found something that was an impossibly lucky find.

A deer carcass.

The meat was mostly gone but there remained a lovely bone. The bone of my dreams.

I scooped it up and lay full length in the waving grass and began an earnest chew. Life was very good.

Almost too good, and so I almost did not

hear the approach of the Indians. If one of them hadn't said something I may not have known they were there until much too late. As it was, they came so suddenly I was forced to abandon my bone and quickly slide into the cover of the woods.

Protected by a deep undergrowth of fern I watched a small group of Indian warriors enter the clearing. They went to the deer carcass and quickly finished dressing it out. They packed the bundles of meat—including my bone—to their backs and turned to leave.

I followed. If there was a chance of getting back my bone, I was going to take it.

They led me to the river. It was a place just around the bend above which Badger and Robair were discarding our disguise. A disguise, I had a feeling, we were going to need again.

All thoughts of bones fled as I looked out from under the cover of an old cedar. Overturned on the bank of the river were more than twenty full-size war canoes. In the shadows of the gathering evening over a hundred Indian warriors were preparing camp.

They were Miamis, allies of the Iroquois.

And by the paint on their bodies, the scalps on their war clubs, and the scent of blood that reached me on the breeze, they were clearly on the warpath.

I watched anxiously as the group returning with the meat melted into the crowd of hostile Indians. This camp was a portage site. The activity of the Indians suggested that they were preparing to portage around a portion of the river ahead where there must be falls or rapids. I began to back away. Robair and Badger had to be warned. But suddenly I caught the thread of a familiar scent and I was frozen to my hiding place.

I lay very still concentrating on the dancing breezes whispering through the cedar overhang of where I crouched. There it was again! But where was it coming from?

And then, two Indian warriors dragged

another, smaller figure stumbling between them. They threw him to the ground near the river only a few yards from where I hid. His hands were bound behind him. They pushed him down and shoved his face into the water until he began to struggle. Laughing they released him and allowed him to drink some water.

The figure, a boy, knelt, wary and exhausted, not trusting his captors, fearful they would suddenly try to drown him again. He quickly took a couple of gulps of water before the warriors kicked him to his feet.

It was Keta.

X

Deathcarrier

When I told Badger about Keta she sat down on the ground and put her face in her hands. I leaned against her knee and after several minutes she reached out and gave me a hug. We—and by that I mean Badger—explained things to Robair.

"They are probably not interested in killing him," said Robair. "It is probably a requickening."

Badger nodded unhappily.

A requickening, I knew, was a practice the Iroquois nations had started not so very long ago.

Tribe numbers had been greatly decreased due to the wars raging and the new diseases brought by the Europeans, especially the deadly smallpox. So now when Iroquois raided or warred on their enemies, instead of killing everybody they took prisoners and tried to convince them to join their tribe. The prisoners really had little choice. Either they agreed to join the tribe or they were killed.

Keta was young enough that this Miami tribe would work extra hard to convince him to join them.

"He will only have been with them for a couple of months," said Robair, trying to reassure Badger.

"We'll have to get him out," she said.

"Okay. Let's think carefully and make a plan," said Robair.

"I could dash in and bite a lot of them while you get Keta," I offered, barking enthusiastically.

"Or we could trade you for the boy," said Archeveque stretching in a melting patch of late afternoon sun. "A demon for an Indian boy seems a fair trade to me."

I chose to ignore him.

"Here's what I think we should do," said Robair to Badger. "You float the disguised canoe down past the encampment. I know that those Indians are going to portage a rough length of the river that is just ahead. It's called Deadman's Rapids. I've had the pleasure of encountering it before. Very nasty. You must be sure, Badger, that you get the canoe to the bank before you get caught in the fast moving water."

Badger nodded. "I can do that."

"Good. The dog and I will find a good place to watch the camp. When it is dark we can sneak in and rescue the boy. We will meet you at the canoe and then we will hide in it until the Indians have passed us on their portage. They won't take time to search for the boy if they are on the warpath."

Badger thought about it for a minute. "Yes," she said at last. "I think it can work."

"Good," said Robair. "Let's get that canoe turned into a snarl of floating driftwood again."

Robair and Badger reassembled the brush and branches over the little birch bark canoe. Badger knelt in the stern and Archeveque pawed and patted at things in the center, looking for just the right spot to settle into. I didn't like that Badger would be alone except for the company of that furry flea kingdom of a cat as she went past the Indian camp. But Archeveque understood that his hide, scruffy as it was, was at stake too. He had hunkered down in the middle of the canoe. Only the slits of his yellow green eyes were visible over the bundles of supplies.

"They'll be okay," said Robair as we stood on the bank and watched the apparent clump of brush and wood debris drift away down the river.

I hoped he was right.

We headed into the woods. It was now late afternoon. The sun was low in the sky and lit the woods in a golden fire. I led him carefully and quietly to the clearing and then on past to a place in the thickness of the trees where we could see the camp.

I scented out at least two warriors on watch. We moved carefully in the underbrush, keeping low, keeping hidden.

In the declining light of the day, the camp was still a busy place. Warriors moved about with purposeful duties. There was no smiling or laughing or joking. All was grim silence except for a few exchanges of words here and there.

Suddenly I could feel Robair tense beside me.

"That's my canoe!" he whispered pointing. Among the turned over canoes there was one that remained at the edge of the water, loaded as if waiting to push off. It was a well-trimmed craft much bigger than Badger's. It had a green band of paint around the rim of it and a sunburst painted on the prow.

Only Robair would be so flamboyant,

I thought.

"That's my canoe!" he said again. "We've got to get it, Pachelot!"

I growled softly to remind him what we were supposed to be doing.

It didn't do any good.

He squirmed and wriggled through the undergrowth in the direction of the canoe. I crouched along with him anxious that the fern and cedar branches he was wiggling through were moving very noticeably should anyone care to suddenly do any of that noticing.

"Robair," I growled urgently. "Stop!"

But then he froze. I became a stone beside him.

Two people had approached the canoe. One was a tall Indian warrior. His hair was carved into a stiff reddish crest at the top of his head leaving most of his scalp clean shaven. Several ragged eagle feathers, fastened somehow in his hair, brushed against the back of his neck as he walked. His face was painted in fierce red streaks. He carried a tomahawk adorned with black beaded streamers.

The other person was a fur trapper. He was a short man with a dark beard. He wore a buckskin shirt fringed with horsehair. He carried a buffalo horn of gunpowder slung over his shoulder, a musket, and a small bundle that, by its smell, was obviously some of the freshly killed deer. He placed both his musket and the meat in the canoe and then turned back to Red Face.

"Segan!" said Robair. "I don't believe it! What's he doing trading with Miamis?"

As we watched, Red Face and Segan were joined by a group of more warriors who made a semi circle around them as the two began to talk. They were talking loudly enough that we could hear them.

Red Face now handed Segan another bundle wrapped in skin.

"Is this it then?" asked Segan.

"Be careful," warned the warrior. "We are

glad to be getting rid of it. It is dangerous and powerful."

Laughing, Segan unwrapped the bundle to reveal a small iron box. Even from where we crouched in the shadows of the woods we could see that it was securely closed with a large iron lock.

"Maybe I should open it just to make sure?" Producing a key from a hidden pocket in his buckskins, Segan held the box out as though he were going to open it. Immediately the Indians surrounding him surged back in what was obviously very great fear.

"What's going on?" whispered Robair. "Why are they frightened?"

Segan was laughing again. "I guess that wouldn't be such a good idea after all," he said and put the key back in his pocket. "After all, this is a gift meant for others, is it not?"

"Why do you not walk around the great rapids with us?" One of the warriors asked. "These waters are guarded by a great Manitou. They are very dangerous."

"I know all about it," Segan said and his tone was mocking. "They call them Deadman's Rapids. But I've been down them before."

The warriors broke into loud, rude laughter.

"You brag too loudly, Deathcarrier," said Red Face. "It would be better to walk around the Loud Waters than to trust them with your life and the weapon you carry. That is a dangerous thing to do."

"Life is dangerous, my friend," said Segan. He carefully wrapped the box in the skin covering and stowed it securely in his canoe.

"But if you drown," said another warrior who was tall and thin and carried a red war club. "You will not be able to carry out your mission."

"I know these rapids," Segan bragged. "I could run them blindfolded and at night. Tell you what. How much do you want to bet that I will make it through them alive? How about ten beaver pelts?"

There was much excited talking among the warriors on this brag.

"Foolish man," muttered Robair.

"We cannot resist the offer of so foolish a man," said Red Face.

"Good!" Segan grinned and quickly yanked a beaded streamer from the tomahawk of Red Face.

Insulted, Red Face raised the weapon, but Segan just laughed again and winked at him.

"I will leave this tied to a stick at the foot of the rapids to prove that I made it."

Red Face lowered his tomahawk. "If you did not have such an important mission to accomplish, Deathcarrier," he said, "I would scalp you where you stand."

"Yes, well, nice exchanging threats with you all," said Segan in a careless tone. "I'll see you all at the fort."

He got into the painted canoe. Next to me Robair gave a little moan and tensed as though he were thinking about leaping out and tackling

Segan on the spot. But then he slumped back as Segan shoved off into the river. There was really nothing he could do with all those tomahawk-carrying Indians standing around.

The canoe rode on the amber water like a jaunty cork in a tub. Segan waved his paddle in the air, gave a war whoop and then began to power down the river.

Several of the warriors whooped back and raced with him running on the bank until they ran out of room and Segan disappeared around the bend.

With a few last, chilling war whoops, Red Face and the other Indian warriors returned to their preparations for portage.

"Wow," Robair exhaled his breath as though he had been holding it. "What is that fool up to? Is he a traitor do you think, Pachelot?"

Yes, that was exactly what I thought.

"I wonder what is so dangerous about that box he carried."

"They named him Deathcarrier," I growled anxiously.

Absently, Robair ran his hand over my head. "Never mind, Pachelot. After we rescue Keta, I will have to go after him. The only fort up that way is one that was built by La Salle a few months back."

La Salle? I wuffed and thumped my tail. Was La Salle in danger then?

"I'll have to get up there and warn them, Pachelot. It seems obvious that La Salle's fort is where these warriors are heading. And by the look of things, the fort may be in serious danger."

XI

The White Beaver

Crickets and other invisible insects began their buzzing chorus as darkness settled in around us. The Indians made no attempt to be hidden. A war party of their size would have little to fear. Fires burned high and then low as the later hours descended. Soon the bundled shadows of warriors lay on the ground in sleep. But which one was Keta?

Robair and I had lain hidden in the darkness of the cedar thicket for several hours after the departure of Segan and scanned the camp, but we had seen no sign of Keta. Every now and then I could catch his scent. I was fairly sure he was somewhere opposite of us and not too far away from the river.

I heard Robair sigh softly next to me. Over the hours we had lain hidden he had turned into a drifted mound of dead leaves that smelled like muskrat. I knew it would be all but impossible for him to creep into that sleeping mass of warriors, try to find Keta, and not get caught.

But I could do it.

"You wait here," I growled. "I can get in, find Keta, and bring him back here."

"You're right," said Robair softly, shaking himself free of the leaves. "It's going to take a lot of careful work for me to get in there."

Obviously the man didn't listen.

"You stay here. Stay now," he said and held his hand in my face.

Stay? What did he think I was, a

trained dog?

Strong measures were called for.

As Robair began to wiggle away I got in his face with all my teeth showing and growled my deepest gurgling growl. He froze.

"Easy, Pachelot," he said. "I know what I'm doing."

But of course he didn't and when he tried to move again I growled some more. Robair might not be the brightest star in the sky, but he eventually got the message. When I was sure he had it, I melted away into the shadows. He did not come after me.

I can be as invisible as the wind if I don't want to be seen. And my nose never lets me down. Moving from patch to patch of deep shadow I found Keta sound asleep near the far edge of the camp, close to the river. He was bound and laying on the ground, but he had no guard over him. Other sleeping warriors lay just feet away, but no one was extremely close to where Keta was.

Softly I crouched down next to him to stay hidden from anyone watching or waking. Even in the darkness I could see his paleness. He was very thin, as well. He was breathing in gasps, but he was asleep. I licked his face. His eyes fluttered open.

"Pachelot? Am I dreaming? Is it really you?" I licked his face again.

"It's me," I thumped my tail against his side.

"Can you get me out of here?"

No problem. I squirmed behind him and the Terror of the Woods used his iron teeth to bite through the ropes in a very short time. Keta had to lie still for a minute until the circulation began to return to his numb hands.

"Badger is with me," I told him. "With any luck she is in her canoe in the river somewhere around here. How about a little swim?"

"My hands are still numb, but they are starting to prick and tingle like tiny needles," said

Keta. "I will need your help."

It was easy to carefully and quietly roll to the edge of the river and then to ease into the water. No one woke up and no one saw us. Like two giant crayfish we crawled away from the shore into the deeper part of the river. As the water became deep enough to swim in, Keta had to grab hold of me by putting his arms around my middle because he was weak and his hands were still mostly useless. In the water I could tow him along with little difficulty. The problem was in which direction should we swim?

All around us the river was a murmuring, moving darkness. There was nothing to guide us. Keta's head rested on my back, but his grip seemed to be firm.

"Hold on," I snorted as water got into my nose a little. At the very least, I would get him to the opposite bank and away from his captors.

But then, suddenly, I spotted a v-ripple of water coming toward me. Some other animal was coasting the river this night. A muskrat maybe? But as it got closer I could tell that it was a very big animal. Something that was much bigger than a muskrat and much bigger than myself. Something more the size of a deer or a bear even. And it was white.

Smoothly it came toward us, the water murmuring a soft ripple in its wake, and then it swerved a little so as to swim by us. As it did, I caught the scent of it.

Beaver!

"Brother Beaver," Keta murmured as if half asleep. "Follow him, Pachelot."

I followed. We swam for what seemed a long time. I stayed in the v-wake of the giant white beaver as it swam silently just ahead of me. I could see the back of its head, which was a whiteness that seemed to glow as if lit by moonlight. Only there wasn't any moon because the clouds were thick in the sky.

Suddenly, I could feel the water quickening

its pace around us. I hoped the giant creature I was following was not going to lead us into the rapids. Keta held on and I towed him along.

And then I saw a clump of river drift just ahead. I could smell Badger and that ratty musty smell that was Archeveque. The giant white shape I had been following disappeared down the river as I towed Keta to Badger's canoe.

She was there and in minutes she had both of us in the canoe, doing the things she needed to be doing to help her brother. He seemed to be almost unconscious, but at least he hadn't drowned.

I poked my head out of the shelter to sniff the breeze. No scent came to me other than that of the muddy waters around us. There was nothing out there now but the murmuring moving darkness that was the river.

"Where is Robair?" Badger asked.

"I'll have to go find him," I said.

"Go," she said. "We'll be okay here."

The canoe was tied to the bank so it was easy

to slip out and into the woods. Later I did have to swim that river again, but I did it in a place above the Indian camp where the river was narrower and very calm. I did not see any giant white beaver. I made my way to the place where I had left Robair.

He wasn't there. Why would he be? The man had very little sense.

I stuck my nose into the breezes and began to search for him.

I finally located him. He had moved down the bank from our hiding place and was now concealed right at the edge of the river. When I crawled up next to him out of the underbrush he jumped a foot or two in the air but, to give him credit, he didn't scream or anything.

"Pachelot!" he whispered. "What are you trying to do to me?"

"Rescue you," I muttered.

"Now don't get grumpy," he said and ruffled my ears. "I knew you would find me."

Grumpy?

"I saw what you did. Very clever. Now, let's get back to Badger and the canoe. Are we going to have to swim?"

For an answer I turned and plunged softly into the water. Robair was not far behind.

"I'm sure swimming at night in very cold river water is good for the circulation," gasped Robair as Badger helped us into the canoe some minutes later. He was dripping water and grinning like he enjoyed being wet.

Keta was wrapped tightly in warm blankets and lay asleep in the bottom of the canoe. I was very displeased to see Archeveque curled on Keta's chest like a sleeping cobra, but then I thought that the creature was probably helping Keta stay warm. So I decided to ignore it.

"Okay," said Robair. "New plan."

"New plan?" asked Badger. "I don't think so. We need to stay right here hidden, warm and safe while my brother has a chance to recover some of his strength."

"I'm sorry," said Robair, "but circumstances have changed. Pachelot and I found Segan as well as Keta. We overheard him talking with the Miamis. Those warriors are on their way to Fort Crevecoeur, just down river from here only a couple of days. When they get there they will take the fort by surprise and massacre everyone there."

"It's a fort," said Badger. "They will have weapons. They can defend themselves."

"Segan is also carrying something else. A weapon or something. The Miamis were very nervous around it. If the fort isn't warned they may not be able to defend themselves."

"It's La Salle's fort," I barked.

"La Salle?" Badger's voice was filled with surprised concern.

"La Salle has built a fort that has become a big trade center in just a short time," said Robair. "So there are whole villages of the Illini tribe gathered around it. The fort is small. They will not be able to defend against this surprise attack."

"We have to warn them," the voice was weak and it belonged to Keta. "Badger, I've listened to them plan it. They are going to kill the women and children as well as the warriors and La Salle and all his men. La Salle will be outnumbered."

"And taken by surprise," added Robair.

"But you are weak," Badger protested. "And anyway how could we beat them there?"

"We leave now," said Robair.

"We can't portage these rapids in the dark," Badger protested.

"We don't have time to portage anyway," said Robair. "Segan has gone ahead. He has a head start and he carries that mysterious weapon. Do you know what it is, Keta?"

"No," Keta murmured from his bundle of blankets. "All I know is that it was something given to the Miamis by a white man who came to trade with them about a month ago. He wasn't happy about La Salle's new center of trade. Whatever it was he gave them, the warriors were deathly afraid of it and couldn't wait to give it to that fur trapper, Segan."

"Okay, but if we don't have time to portage," said Badger, "what are you suggesting?"

There was a small silence. We all knew the answer to that question, but it was the weak voice of Keta that answered.

"We have to run the rapids," he said. "And we have to go now."

XII

Deadman's Rapids

The cloud cover began to give way and a weak glimmer of moonlight made ghostly shapes of the dark trees around us. Working quickly, we once again uncovered Badger's canoe revealing the slender and small birch bark craft for what it was. It was a tight fit for all of us. Keta remained sitting in the middle of the canoe with me across his knees. Badger knelt in the bow and carried her paddle at the ready. When we entered the rapids it would be her job to call out the rocks and fend us off if we got too close.

Although, in the darkness of the night, even if the moonlight stayed with us, I did not know how we would see any rocks at all until we were testing the strength of them against our bodies.

Robair took up a position in the stern of the canoe. His strength would paddle us through and keep us from flipping broadside to the current, which would result in our tipping over. Archeveque crouched low in front of him, iron claws secured in the skin of the canoe itself.

We had to leave some of Badger's supplies behind to make enough room for all of us. Robair made a cache for her at the base of a white pine that would be easy to find again if we came back this way. The supplies were wrapped up tightly and buried. No one would find them.

As we eased the canoe out onto the river Robair called for us to wait while he made an offering to La Vieille, the old woman of the wind. He took a twist of tobacco from his pocket and tossed it into the river.

"Segan has my pipe as well as my canoe," he said with a shrug. "But La Vieille likes a little tobacco now and then. May she protect our voyage."

And he took up his paddle to move us swiftly into the current of the dark water.

"There are others looking out for us as well. Right, Pachelot?" said Keta softly, and ran his battered hand through my fur.

"Right," I wuffed back to him remembering the giant white beaver that had helped us find Badger.

"Don't tell me you can talk to that dog too," moaned Robair.

Keta laughed.

"Don't worry," I heard Archeveque mutter from the shadows in the rear. "It's not like he has a lot to say."

Then suddenly the rumble of heavy rapids reached us and the river began to pick up an extremely fast pace indeed.

"Here we go!" shouted Robair and he began to paddle very hard.

Surprisingly, Robair seemed to know what he was doing. It was almost completely dark except for the glimmering thread of soft moonlight that dimly illuminated the river.

The roar of rushing water was deafening. These were not just little rapids. Soon the water was boiling around us in a churning frenzy of violence.

"Look sharp!" Robair called to Badger.

Robair had called this stretch of the river Deadman's Rapids. There could only be one reason why they were called that.

We entered the first stretch of rapids at full speed. It was a long and violent path of watery turmoil. Huge trunks of black trees were rammed along the riverbank, but there did not seem to be much in the way of obstacles in the center of the boiling water.

"Sharp turn ahead!" called out Badger.

"Okay!" Robair answered her. "I remember this one!" He said more quietly. But both Keta and I heard him and heard the tension in his voice. Keta reached out and got a firm grip on me.

"Hold on, my friend," he said.

As we stormed up to the sharp turn, the wild, cold darkness around us was a blur of chaos and confusion. Robair expertly back paddled slowing us as much as his strength, pitted against that of the river, would allow.

It was enough.

The little canoe swerved neatly around the bend. The bow tilted up and then slammed down as we lurched over a small fall. We were drenched in an icy spray of water.

"Rock! Dead ahead!" Badger screamed.

Standing waves on either side threatened to engulf us. Robair paddled like a mad man and we swerved by the rock that was as big as a small wigwam. Eddies boiled around the sides of the black monster, but we were past it before anyone could even think about it.

"Port side!" Badger yelled.

Robair maneuvered. We slammed over another series of low falls, narrowly avoiding rocks. Once we brushed too close to a small black boulder shouldering out of the seething water. Badger struck out with her paddle in a jarring impact, but managed to fend us off.

The river convulsed and threw us forward into the last long stretch. This area was filled with debris and rocks. Badger frantically called them out as she spotted them. Robair responded with powerful strokes of his paddle, which seemed, sometimes, to be so strong that they lifted the little craft clean out of the water.

Then the frenzied river began to dimple into small runs of pattering rills. The roar of boiling water was behind us. Soaked and shocked we sat in the canoe, almost unable to breathe as we swirled into smoother and smoother water.

At last, Robair paddled us to the bank.

Badger tied us up to an overhanging branch and we all sat as though bewildered that we had made it.

Finally, Robair broke the silence. "Those blue eyes of yours saw everything, Badger. Without your sharp sight we would never have made that run."

"You've made that run before," said Keta quietly.

Robair did not answer at once. Then he said, "Yes. On a voyager's bet. A race. My partner fell over and was drowned. I never thought I would be so stupid as to find myself on that killer stretch of river again, let alone in the dark."

"It was odd," said Badger from the dimness of the bow. "Those rocks all had a sort of whiteness about them that made it easy for me to see them. It was as though they were being illuminated by the moon. They must reflect moonlight somehow."

I felt Keta's hands tighten in my fur. Not moonlight, we knew, but something more powerful and much more mysterious.

Robair hauled Archeveque from his hiding place and fed him some bits of dried fish. He began talking to him in that silly way, calling him a pirate and petting that vile head as though he liked doing it. Badger saw to it that Keta got a dose of her medicine and that we all got some food as well.

As we were munching pemmican and dried corn, I caught the drift of scent from something on the bank just down from us.

"There's something there," I wuffed to Keta.

Keta straightened up in the canoe and peered into the gloom. "Oh, I see it," he said. "It's a stick of some kind and there seems to be a streamer of shiny things on it."

"Beads," said Robair. "Segan's marker. He must have made it through the rapids then."

"Well, we are going to be the only ones to know it," said Badger. "Look."

She pointed and now we could see a small furry shape trundling along the edge of the shore.

It was a beaver out doing its nightly work. The animal snuffled along until it found Segan's marker and then, in one quick snap of its jaws, it snatched up the stick and began carrying it off.

Robair laughed. "The fool! He hung his message on a green stick. That beaver has just been handed a delicious snack for a late dinner." He roared with laughter and the little canoe shook as though it were back in the clutch of the rapids.

After resting for several more minutes, Robair pushed us back into the current of the river. He was anxious to try and overtake Segan and wanted to keep moving. Keta said he was okay and could handle it, so Badger allowed it.

Dawn found us several miles further along. The air misted into view around us as birds began to chatter in the trees. The woods on either side were a blaze of color still, but the cold chill in the air spoke clearly of winter winds not too far behind.

Sometime in mid-morning Badger spied an

overhang covered with wild grapes. Robair steered the canoe under the shaded canopy of the fallen tree and Badger harvested some of the fruit for us without even leaving the canoe. Of course, I'm not big on fruit myself, but Keta seemed to enjoy it.

I watched him gobble the purple fruit in handfuls, grinning widely as he did so.

I barked absentmindedly at a squirrel that chattered insults at us from overhead.

"The bones of that scrawny creature are too small for you," Robair said to me. "But if we catch up to Segan and I can get my canoe back, I promise to give you a bone worthy of your dreams. I have one, you see. It's a soup bone. And it's yours if we can get it."

So I sort of forgave the old muskrat bean for assuming the Terror of the Woods would stoop to munching squirrel bones. Archeveque, of course, had no such scruples and when Robair wasn't paying attention he swagged up that tree shredding dead bark under his strong claws going after that squirrel like wind ripping through leaves.

There were several interesting moments of daring acrobatics as the squirrel led the cat spiraling higher and higher into the ever thinning branches of the dead overhang. And it ended with Archeveque making one final, magnificent leap straight at the annoyance with the flicking tail only to find, not squirrel, but dead branch which gave beneath his weight and dropped him like a squalling stone straight into the water.

I don't know—I thought it was funny.

XIII

The Revenge of Ahanu

We were three days on the river. We often found signs of Segan moving ahead of us, but he was moving faster and we could never seem to catch up with him. This made Robair grumpy. Badger's canoe was a bit small for him. He crouched in the stern with his knobby knees almost up around his ears and that obnoxious cat, Archeveque, curled on his feet like some moth eaten old blanket.

Sometimes Robair muttered to himself about interesting things like pulverized liver and crunchy bones. I think he was composing recipes.

Badger took good care of Keta and he was gradually regaining his strength. He slept or rested in the middle of the canoe. I stretched out next to him or sometimes I sprawled across his knees to keep him warm. He seemed to suffer chills and shaking.

When he was feeling better, he told us about his adventures.

"I saw you go overboard," Keta said to me one afternoon as Robair paddled, Archeveque slept, and Badger rested in the bow.

Keta and I had been dozing in the golden light of midday. It was pleasant on the smooth, glassy surface of the river and hard to remember the dark fear of those final moments aboard the *Griffon*.

"I tossed the bucket out to you hoping that you would be able to swim to it."

"I did!" I barked. "It saved my life."

Keta ruffled my ears. I liked it when he did

that, although I would never stoop to a rattling purr like some other, less well-mannered, creatures I could name.

"I never saw what happened," he said. "I was trying to secure my canoe to the deck when the rope broke. So I just jumped into it before it went overboard. A big wave smashed over the side of the ship and washed us off the deck. I was able to grab a paddle and so, for a while, I could keep us afloat among those mountains of waves. It was terrifying."

"Us? Who else was with you?" asked Robair.

"The cat," said Keta. "He had been taking a nap in my supplies when the storm struck. He didn't have a chance to leave."

"Poor old pirate," murmured the demented Robair as he stroked the furry alligator on his head. Archeveque, in the staked out territory between Robair's feet, rested his chin on one of Robair's stolen moccasins and sat on the other.

Maybe if you smelled a little like brother skunk yourself you didn't tend to notice the strong smells of others. I swear the smell from Robair's feet could wilt grass. But then, perhaps, I'm a bit oversensitive in the nose area.

"And then what?" asked Badger.

"Well," said Keta. "Then we just washed ashore somewhere. We were both exhausted. My canoe was done for. Its back was broken. I think the cat was half drowned and we both sort of just passed out. When we woke up, we found ourselves surrounded by that war band of Miami.

"They took me right away and wanted me to join their tribe. It was a rough time. When we came into the territory of the Amikwa, I told Archeveque to go and find safety there. The Miami didn't like him and sometimes they threw spears at him in sport trying to kill him."

Interesting, I thought. I never imagined I would sympathize with hostile Indians.

"I know what you are thinking, bone breath,"

said Archeveque from his moccasin bed. "Just remember that some Indians eat dog."

He had a point.

"I kept hoping," Keta continued, "I could escape somehow, but I wasn't getting the chance."

"Did you hear anything else about their plans?" Robair wanted to know.

"Only that they were planning on joining up with a bigger band of Senecas, and then attack Fort Crevecoeur."

"Why?" Badger asked.

Keta shrugged. "They never exactly said."

"Revenge," Robair told her. "There are complex politics at work. The Illini are hunting beaver in the lands claimed by the Iroquois nations. They are taking a lot of the beaver. I have heard that they are even hunting the young beaver."

"That's bad," said Keta, pulling the blankets tighter under his chin. The sunny air was still chilly. "There won't be any beaver for the next season if they take the young like that."

"A few months ago the Seneca leader, Annanhaa, was trying to seek a diplomatic solution to all this hunting." Robair rested his paddle on his knees. Water dripped in a slow rhythm from its edge. "He was murdered by the Illini."

"This war party is the revenge, then," said Keta.

Robair sent the canoe smoothly ahead with several powerful strokes.

"How many warriors do you think there will be when the Miami join the main force?" asked Badger over her shoulder.

"From what I heard," answered Keta quietly, "over five hundred."

There was a sort of stifled gasp from Robair. He began to paddle faster.

At night we had to stop and camp. Badger insisted that everyone needed to rest, especially Keta, but I think she also knew that, strong as he was, Robair could not paddle forever without rest and food.

Robair tilted the canoe up on its side and built a small campfire in front of it. The heat built up and was captured by the pocket of the canoe and then reflected back.

Nighttime was when Archeveque woke up. After begging as much food from Robair as he could, the yellow menace would disappear into the night to hunt. He was always back, though, before the chill of the deep night set in, finding his way into Robair's blankets where he could be warm.

One night Keta asked Badger if she would tell us a story. Robair had been restlessly pacing back and forth to the water. He hated it when we had to stop. The cat had disappeared into the night. Everyone seemed a bit on edge. A story would be a good idea.

"Any one in particular?" asked Badger.

"Ahanu and the Beaver People," said Keta.

Badger sat still for a moment as she collected her thoughts. Sparks drifted up into the darkness above the fire and ignited with sharp snaps. A breeze played along the riverbank and I could smell the old scent of deer.

"I wish I had my pipe," complained Robair as he came to sit beside the fire to listen.

"I wish I had a bone to crunch," I growled in sympathy.

Robair shot a suspicious look in my direction. "Is he complaining too?" he asked.

Keta laughed, one of the few times I had heard him do so since his rescue. "Bones," he said.

"Be patient, my friend," said Robair to me. "I promise, when we get back my canoe you will have your bone and I will have my pipe! You leave it to me. I'm thinking up nice little revenge strategies."

"Revenge is what Ahanu wanted too," said Badger beginning her story at last. "Ahanu was the young chief of a small village over the hills, closer to where the sun sets. In his land it was always warm. Rivers and lakes of blue water were everywhere, and food was plentiful.

"Ahanu loved to laugh and play games. He taught his warriors a new game everyday. In the evenings the clan sat around the fire and told stories and sang songs. They were very happy and had nothing to worry about—until the day Winter came.

"Ahanu's village woke up one morning to discover everything covered in a thick blanket of snow and ice. Winter sat in the middle of their village, a cruel smile on his face and mocked Ahanu's people.

"Ahanu called to his warriors to rid the village of this unwanted guest, but the warriors only knew games and could do nothing.

"'He will go away if we ignore him,' said Ahanu.

"But the children were cold and the people were hungry. There was no food and the blue lakes and rivers were white with ice and snow. The people began to be afraid.

"'You must go and find help,' said the people

to Ahanu. 'You must go and find some way to get rid of Winter.'

"So Ahanu left his village to try and find some way to save them.

"He was not laughing now.

"He walked many days and many dark and cold nights. Winter was everywhere. The snow was deep, but he struggled on. Then he came to a lake frozen over with Winter's ice. In the middle of the lake there rested a hut made of sticks and wood.

"'Who has a wigwam in the middle of a lake?' Ahanu wondered. And he went to investigate.

"He found a door in the side of the hut and he opened it and went inside. There he discovered a very old man whose long white beard and hair covered his face and head. The old man was sitting on the floor and he seemed to be waiting.

"'Have you seen my sons?' asked the old man when Ahanu entered.

"'No,' answered Ahanu. 'I have only seen

Winter.'

"'My sons are hunting,' said the old man. 'When they return we will have a feast. Sit down and wait with me if you will.'

"So Ahanu, feeling the rumbling of his empty stomach, sat down and waited with the old man. While he waited, the old man began to sing. Ahanu listened to the strange songs and learned many things from them. He learned about work and planting. He listened to the song of hunters and the song of the wild rice. He heard the cry of distant birds and learned of travel, the song of finding. He learned the song of fire and warmth.

"'These songs are a gift to you,' said the old man.

"'Thank you,' said Ahanu. 'I have learned many things, but can you teach me how to get rid of Winter?'

"'No,' said the old man. When he looked at Ahanu his eyes were a shiny black like dark pools of shadowed water. 'No one knows how to get rid of Winter.'

"When the sons of the old man returned they brought with them much food. Ahanu ate as much as he could hold and then fell asleep.

"When he woke up in the morning he was alone in the hut. He crawled out and found his way back to his village. There he taught his people the songs that were the gift of the old man.

"The first thing Ahanu's people did was to make fire and get warm. When they were warm, they wanted food for their hunger.

"Ahanu had told them about the wigwam in the middle of the lake and of the feast the sons of the old man gave him.

"'We must go there and get some of the food for ourselves,' said the people.

"'No,' said Ahanu. 'I have taught you the songs of hunting. You must go and hunt for yourself. We must not bother the old man and his sons.'

"But the people of his village did not listen

and they left to find the old man and the wigwam in the middle of the frozen lake.

"Ahanu would not show them the way but they followed his tracks in the snow and found the lake. When they ran out to the wigwam, which was really, they saw, just a hut of sticks and wood, they could not find a door.

"They yelled for the old man to come out and threw chunks of ice at the hut. No one appeared.

"But as they turned away to leave they heard a noise behind them. Looking back they saw a giant white beaver sitting on the roof of the hut. Just then they saw two smaller beavers hurrying across the frozen lake toward the hut dragging some small trees with them.

"The people, remembering the hunting songs Ahanu had taught them, killed the two beavers and took them back to the village to eat.

"Ahanu could do nothing to stop them and they left him alone on the frozen lake.

"The giant white beaver looked at him and its

eyes were a shiny black like dark pools of shadowed water.

"The next day Winter left Ahanu's village. When Ahanu returned he found all his people sick and dying. In despair he made a large spear and set out to find the white beaver."

Badger stopped talking. The fire popped sparks.

"Is that the end of the story?" Robair demanded.

Badger nodded.

"Well, that's no good!"

"Why not?" asked Badger. "What more do you want to know?"

"Well, for starters, did Ahanu ever find the beaver? And then I want to know if he got his revenge. And then I want to know what happened to him after that. For crying out loud," Robair smacked his palm on the ground, "that is not a finished story!"

"No," said Keta quietly. "And that's the

point. It isn't finished. Ahanu is still looking."

Robair was quiet while he thought about it. "You mean there is never any satisfaction in revenge, I suppose. Well, that's too bad, because when I catch up to that skunk who stole my canoe, my tobacco, and my musket I don't plan on shaking his hand."

"I would have liked the story better if it had been about a bone," I growled softly.

"See?" said Robair. "The dog agrees with me." And he turned over rolling himself up in his blanket. After a few minutes he began to snore.

I thought Keta had fallen asleep too, but then he spoke. "Badger, that story is about something else too, isn't it?"

"I always thought so," Badger agreed.

"Bones?" I suggested.

Keta reached over and ran his hand through my coat. "No, Pachelot. I think it has something to do with caring for the things that care for you. The Beaver Man gave Ahanu powerful medicine. In return, Ahanu's people should have honored him. Instead they killed his only sons."

"It's betrayal," Badger agreed.

Somewhere in the distant night a wolf sent up a shivery howl. We crowded close to the dying fire. The thought of the man who would betray the Indians at LaSalle's fort was heavy in our hearts. Would we be able to catch Segan before he used the mysterious weapon he carried in the iron box?

XIV

Fort Crevecoeur

The next morning Archeveque was back in a curled twiggy ball in Robair's blanket and there was a skiff of ice at the edge of the river. Shivering in the gray chill of early, early morning, we loaded the canoe and pushed off.

Robair took long and powerful strokes with his paddle. On each stroke he sent a loud complaint into the still river air around us.

"I want my pipe!" he shouted, startling a blue jay resting on a dead overhang on the riverbank.

"I want my canoe!" he bellowed next, with a wild stroke that sent a spray of water into the air.

"And even though it doesn't shoot straight, I want my musket!" This was answered by a sharp slap on the water and we all looked up to see a beaver swimming quickly away, a rippled V in its wake.

Robair laughed and the canoe rocked crazily from side to side. "I want all the world to know it!"

"I think all the world does," said Badger clutching the edge of the canoe. "So will you please settle down now before you dump us all in the water?"

"A brisk swim in cold as death water is good for you," said Robair. "Just ask me, I should know!"

And nothing seemed to be able to shake the boisterous mood he was in. As the sun began to brighten the air around us, Robair began to sing. Finally Badger gave up trying to keep up with his vigorous paddling and took out her flute and played along. I decided to add my best singing voice too and accompanied them with a sort of howly yipping I had learned from listening to coyotes one night.

The song went something like this:

My canoe and my pipe are my friends for life.
My musket will bring home dinner.
I'll travel the river from dawn to dusk
Faster than any man ever.

I think that Robair was making it up as he went along, but then, so was I. I think we sounded good.

Keta covered his ears but he was laughing too.

The more barbaric element among us, of course, was not only unappreciative of our harmonizing, but downright rude about it.

"Stop it!" Archeveque hissed. "You sound as though you are murdering a goose!"

We ignored him and the old yellow menace finally hissed his way completely under a blanket where he became an irritated brown lump with a thorny attitude. Robair, unfortunately, discovered this attitude when he tried to pick him up and found he was holding a spiky furred ball of fury with very sharp claws.

"Ouch!" yelled Robair, and instead of tossing the fleabag into the river, as he should have done, he dropped Archeveque with an angry thump back to the bottom of the canoe.

Robair was a slow learner, that was obvious.

A few hours later Robair, possibly tired from singing, began asking Keta some questions.

"What kind of man is this La Salle?" he wanted to know.

"He's a good friend and a very smart man!" I barked enthusiastically.

"Does Pachelot know him?" asked Robair sounding surprised.

"Yes," said Keta. "It was Pachelot who introduced us. La Salle is a good man."

Robair was silent for a moment. "I'm a *coureur-de-bois*," he said sounding serious. "A woods runner. And, just now, due to the rules of the new governor, all the woods runners are considered outlaws. "

"The way I've always heard it," said Keta, "is that La Salle is a fair man. Pachelot has told me of times when La Salle and Tonti, his lieutenant, often sought the advice of the woods runners."

"Well, let's hope that is still so," said Robair. "It may come down to my word against Segan's."

"*Our* word against Segan's," I barked.

"Did he say he would bite that hairy thief for me?" asked Robair.

Keta laughed.

We reached the fort later that morning. Keta was dozing. Robair had sung himself hoarse and Archeveque was still hiding under his blanket.

"There it is!" said Badger excitedly.

La Salle had named this outpost in the wilderness Fort Crevecoeur, which in French means Fort Brokenheart. I thought that losing the *Griffon* must have been the thing that had broken his heart.

Robair dug into the water with his paddle and the little canoe shot swiftly ahead.

The fort was built on a hill overlooking the river. Two ravines cut deeply along either side of it. La Salle had further built up the defenses by the construction of a *chevaux-de-frise* along the border of the ravines. This was a series of heavy timbers in a line laced with diagonal timbers tipped with spikes. The landscape around the fort was bare of trees. It looked like it was ready to handle an attack.

On the opposite side of the river from the fort spread a substantial Indian village.

Robair brought us to the bank on the fort side. A man came forward to greet us and help to pull the canoe onto the bank. Just down from where we landed we could see a large gathering of people. Robair tried to keep the canoe steady as Badger got out, but the crowd distracted him. Looking over his shoulder he was trying to see what all the commotion was about.

Carefully, Badger helped Keta from the canoe. I stayed crouched down waiting for him to get out first. Suddenly, Archeveque streaked out from under his blanket and bolted ashore.

The man helping us out laughed. "Cats don't like water much," he chuckled. "Where you folks from?"

"We've just come down the river," said Badger. "We need to see Sieur de La Salle immediately. We have some important information for him."

"Well, La Salle is gone, little miss," said the man. "He's on his way back to Quebec. Left about a week ago."

"Who is in charge then?" asked Keta.

"I'm thinking you probably want to speak

with Iron Hand Tonti," said the man.

Suddenly a roar went up from the crowd on the riverbank.

"Say," said Robair. "Just what is going on down there?"

"Oh that!" the man laughed. "That there is a canoe race, friend. Tonti's got a bet of a pouch of first rate tobacco that his canoe can beat any challengers. I don't know why..."

But what he had to say was left unfinished as Robair suddenly, violently shoved the little canoe back into the water. He began back paddling furiously, propelling us back out into the river.

And by that I mean, Robair and me. Badger and Keta stood openmouthed on the bank and, of course, the cat was long gone.

"Robair!" Badger shouted. "Where are you going?"

"Yes!" I barked. "Where are we going?"

"Pachelot!" Robair shouted. "Get in the bow of the canoe to balance me. There isn't a canoe race I haven't won! We're going in!"

And by that he meant we would be joining the race, but his powerful strokes on the little canoe just about pitched us *in* the river.

I quickly jumped up to the bow of the boat and sat with the breeze in my face. The power of Robair's paddling created a wind that blew my ears back a bit. I panted showing a lot of teeth. I could tell that this was going to be great excitement!

I barked as much to him. Robair laughed.

Somewhere ahead of us there was a bang of a musket. The smell of gunpowder drifted back to me.

"It's the start of the race!" Robair yelled. He dug deep into the river with another stroke that was so powerful it almost elevated the little canoe out of the water.

We surged ahead. As we came around the slight curve of the bank we began to pass the crowd, which didn't see us until we had catapulted past. We could only hear their shouts and questions at our back. Robair grinned and bent to the pull of his paddle through the muddying water.

In the river up ahead there were a dozen or so canoes. Many had two men in them paddling together. There was a lot of laughing and yelling between the competitors. Water sprayed into the air with shouts and curses. Suddenly, one canoe tumbled over, spilling its men into the river.

We shot past as they spluttered and splashed to the surface.

Soon we began passing canoes. Robair was a fiend in the stern of Badger's small canoe. He dug into the water sending the canoe swiftly forward as though we were flying. We passed one canoe after another. Some men shouted after us, but Robair ignored them. His teeth showed in a determined grin through the scraggle of his black beard. His eyes were on the lead canoes.

There were three of them.

We passed close to a canoe of two men, one big and fat, the other small and loud.

"Look out, you cross-eyed turkey!" shouted the small man as we zoomed past them, our wake rocking their boat. "Is he paddling that thing or are they flying?" We heard him say to his fat partner as we left them behind.

Soon, the only canoes ahead of us were the three lead canoes.

The canoe in the rear was being paddled by one man who was shouting wildly as his paddle flashed in and out of the water. The breeze blowing in my face suddenly brought me his scent and I began barking furiously. I recognized that scent! It was one I would never forget!

"That's right, Pachelot!" shouted Robair. "Let them know we're coming! We'll catch them all!"

We pulled even with the third place canoe. I looked over at the wild man paddling it and grinned at him. His hair was a tangled mess of blowing fury. His raggedy clothes slashed and danced about him with the movements of his frantic paddling.

It was Stinky Henri!

He looked over at me and his eyes widened in surprise.

I barked at him.

"Zat is ze crazy dog again!" he yelled. "Ze dog who chase me into ze tree! I dream bad dreams about you, Crazy Dog! You are always chasing and biting Henri!"

"You chased that man into a tree?" asked Robair.

"I have my moments!" I barked.

"And now he beat me in ze canoe?" Stinky Henri was having a hard time paddling now and coping with his surprise at the same time. "Unbelievable!" Finally he settled for shaking his paddle at us as we catapulted by him.

"Okay, Pachelot," said Robair. "Look sharp now, there's the man we want!"

At first I thought he meant Iron Hand Tonti. That was who was in the next canoe. Tonti was paddling with long, even, powerful strokes and he was gaining on the canoe ahead of him.

But it wasn't Tonti Robair had his eye on. It was the man in the first canoe, a beautiful craft with sleek lines, a painted green stripe around the top of it and a sunburst painted on the prow.

Segan.

And then something about Robair changed. He was no longer just a man trying to win a canoe race. Now he was a man trying to catch a thief and dangerous outlaw.

We surged past Tonti as though he were merely floating still in the river.

"Pachelot!?" he cried as we skimmed by. "Pachelot! Is that you?"

I barked as enthusiastic a greeting as I could without actually leaping into the water and swimming to him—which is what I wanted to do.

I heard him laugh and he bent his back to the paddling. Tonti knew he wasn't going to win, but he wasn't, like Stinky Henri, going to give up.

Ahead of us Segan was unaware of who his

challenger was. Robair paddled furiously and soon we pulled even. When Segan glanced over and saw it was Robair, he missed a stroke in the water and almost fell in.

"Robair!" he shouted. "Nice of you to join me. I wondered how long you were going to lay about with those Indians!"

"Segan," Robair growled back sounding almost like me. "Nice canoe."

And it was a nice canoe. It was Robair's.

Segan laughed. "Well, if you want it, you will have to catch me first!"

And with that he veered away from the straight ahead course of the race and headed for the riverbank. Robair meant to follow him but he made the adjustment too quick for Badger's little canoe and the craft flipped over spilling us both into the boiling, choking water.

XV

The Iron Box

I bobbed to the surface and looked around for Robair. I saw him at once swimming powerfully after Segan. The thief in the canoe had the advantage, of course, and was fast out-distancing the swimming Robair.

Suddenly Tonti was beside me in his canoe. He reached down with his good hand and helped me to scramble in.

"Pachelot!" I sprayed him with water as I shook out my coat, rocking his canoe dangerously.

"I never thought I would see you again!"

I enthusiastically licked his face, wiggling my joy at seeing him too. "What's going on?" he asked.

"Thief! Thief!" I barked, pointing my nose toward the bank where, even now, Segan was beaching the canoe.

Tonti recognized that word all right. "Really?" he said, and began to paddle powerfully toward shore.

Soon we overtook the thrashing, swimming Robair. And by that I mean, if a half drowning bear were trying to swim, that would have been the scraggly *coureur-de-bois*. To be fair, he had been paddling half a day and had, in fact, just won a very competitive canoe race—sort of—and so was, perhaps, just a tiny bit exhausted as he tried to swim after his long sought enemy. Who was, unfortunately, getting away.

"Let me help you into the canoe!" Tonti shouted at him. But Robair, swimming furiously, ignored him. Maybe he had water in his ears making him deaf. Or maybe he just didn't want to stop. Maybe he couldn't.

"Stop swimming!" Tonti commanded.

And he did. And promptly sank like a stone.

When he spluttered and spat back to the surface, Iron Hand Tonti snagged the back of his shirt with his iron hand and hauled him into the canoe like a giant hooked fish.

Robair lay gasping and choking in the bottom of the canoe with river water running into his eyes and streaming from his beard. "We must stop that man," he gasped out at last.

"So I gather," said Tonti, calmly, taking up his paddle again.

Tonti's strong paddling brought us to the bank and Robair's abandoned canoe. Before Tonti had even landed, Robair leaped into the shallow water and splashed, staggering ashore. Tonti pulled his canoe onto the beach and joined Robair where the *coureur-de-bois* was wildly searching through his canoe.

"What is going on here?" asked Tonti, hands on his hips.

"This is my canoe," said Robair. "Aha!" He had found his pipe and a big smile creased his face. "And now for the tobacco."

Tonti and I watched in silence as Robair engaged in more frenzied searching which, at last, yielded a pouch of tobacco. He plopped himself down in the mud by the river and proceeded to light it.

Tonti watched him in silence trying to decide whether or not he had rescued a crazy man. I understood that feeling. When it came to Robair, crazy was a word you found yourself often considering.

"What about Segan?" I barked, dancing to the edge of the thick cover of trees edging the riverbank.

"Oh, yes, of course," said Robair smacking

himself on the forehead. Wreaths of smoke poured from his slender pipe as he puffed furiously and, once again, leaped to his feet to rummage in his canoe. This time his search produced a small bulky package wrapped tightly in oilcloth. Carefully, Robair cut the twine holding the cloth in place and unwrapped—a bone!

And what a bone it was.

The smell of it hit my nose and it was like rolling in the best smelling things you could imagine. I felt the fur tingle along my legs and my tail began to wave like a flag in the wind. The darkness of the woods, the escaping thief, all was forgotten in that delicious moment.

"Here you go, my friend," said Robair, tossing the bone to me.

I caught it out of the air and it chunked into my mouth in a most satisfying way. Happily, I plopped down in the mud right next to Robair and his smelly pipe and began a blissful gnawing.

"Well, I never," said Tonti shaking his head.

"My best soup bone," said Robair, grinning through puffs of smoke. "I promised it to Pachelot when we got my canoe back."

"What about the man that stole it from you?" asked Tonti. "Shouldn't we go after him?"

"I'll catch up to him someday," said Robair. "He still has my musket. It's not a very straight shooting musket, you understand. But it's mine and I want it back. Just now, however, I have something more important to tell you."

And Robair, not smiling now, told Tonti about the Indian war party that was on its way to attack Fort Crevecoeur.

Under the tan and sunburn of his face, Tonti turned pale.

"What's wrong?" asked Robair. "We saw the fort. You can hold out against them."

"Normally, we could," said Tonti. "But just now over half of the Illini warriors from the village are gone on a religious festival observance. We have only the women and children and some of the old men too elderly to make the pilgrimage. La Salle has just left and he took some more of the men with him.

"Robair, we only have about forty men to defend that fort!"

We returned to the fort shortly after that. Tonti went at once to confer with his men and the Indian leaders left in charge of the village. Robair and I went in search of Keta and Badger.

We found them in the fort surrounded by a small gathering of Indian children. With them was Stinky Henri.

"Oh no! Ze vicious dog!" he said when he saw me. He stood up as though he were going to run away, but Badger put a hand on his arm.

"It's okay, Henri. Pachelot won't hurt you."

I set my bone on the ground at my feet and cocked my head at him, pushing my ears forward. I smiled. He looked nervously at my teeth.

Trust me, some people just never learn

the difference between a smile and a threatening grimace. He sat back down, keeping an eye on me, and went back to the whittling he had been doing when we appeared.

I picked up my bone and went to lie next to Keta, but I continued to watch Stinky Henri too. Just out of curiosity. I wanted to see if the spiders were still living on him.

"What's going on here?" asked Robair.

"Henri is making whistles for the children and Badger is trying to teach them how to play," said Keta, a big smile on his face.

A ring of children ranging in age from about three human years to seven sat in the dust around Keta and Badger. Stinky Henri, using a small, almost completely rusted knife, was busy carving and whittling small sticks and handing them out to the children.

Sitting on Keta's knee was a small Indian girl. Her buckskin dress was very dirty and she had smudges of dirt on her face. Her pudgy little hands were tightly holding a slender willow whistle.

"This is Alawa," introduced Keta. "She is trying to learn how to play the chickadee call."

Alawa gave Robair a shy smile. Then she puckered up her mouth, making two tiny dimples appear in her cheeks, put the whistle to her lips, and gave a vigorous blow. It sounded like a small wind caught in a doorway.

Robair laughed. "Keep trying, little sweet-pea," he said.

"Did you capture Segan?" Badger asked.

"No," said Robair. "He got away, but I got my canoe back."

"And Pachelot got his bone, I see," she said.

I growled appreciatively as I mauled my treasure. Stinky Henri almost cut his finger off as I did. Alawa screamed a baby laugh and blew on her whistle this time producing a thin shrieky sound, which surprised her. She squirmed on Keta's knee and laughed again.

"What about the iron box?" asked Keta

holding onto Alawa to keep her from tumbling to the ground.

"What iron box?" It was Tonti. He came to stand by us watching the children but not really seeing them. He was frowning.

"Segan had an iron box the Miami gave him," explained Robair. "They said it contained a weapon. They seemed very nervous about it."

"These were the Indians that held you captive?" Tonti asked Keta.

"Yes," said Keta. "But I don't know what was in the box."

"I do," said Stinky Henri.

We all looked at him in surprise.

"What?" he asked irritably. "I know a few zings. I zink I know what was in ze box. How big was it, zis box?"

"Not big," said Keta. He held up his hands to measure how big the box was. "Not heavy either. It was locked and made of metal."

"I have seen one like zis before," said

184

Stinky Henri.

"What was it?" asked Tonti.

"Once when I paddled to the *pays de haut* with ze voyagers, we came upon an Indian village. All ze people were gone. Crops were rotting in ze fields and only ghosts were in ze empty wigwams. Ze Indians, they all dead, you see? They all die from a mysterious disease brought to them by zis white men.

"We did not stop to look in the village, but as we paddle by we see zis small iron box sitting at the edge of ze village. It is surrounded by powerful medicine totems, but it is no use. Ze box, it is open. Ze monster has been turned loose."

"Smallpox," said Tonti, his voice rough with rage. "Segan is carrying a box of smallpox contamination."

"And with it," said Stinky Henri, "he is planning ze deaths of many peoples."

XVI

The Strategy Of Delay

"Well," said Robair. "I'll have to go after him."

"Wait," said Tonti. "We have another problem here. We don't have enough men to defend the fort. We have decided to abandon it."

"And go where?" demanded Robair.

"There is a natural fortress we can go to. It is a rock outcropping not far from here. A few men can hold it indefinitely against any number of attackers."

"How long will it take to get there?" asked Keta.

"About a half a day," said Tonti. "We are starting now. But there is one other thing."

"What is it?" asked Badger, her blue eyes looked serious.

"The Indians do not want to risk the women and children in the new fortress. I think they will be safe there, but I cannot convince the Indian leaders of this. Instead they want to take the women and children and hide them on an island in a lake just up the river."

"How far up the river?" asked Robair.

"Two days overland," answered Tonti quietly.

"Two days!" Robair was angry. "The war party will be here by then!"

"I know," said Tonti. "That's why I've devised a strategy to hopefully delay them."

"Why do I have a bad feeling about this?" asked Robair.

"What is your plan?" asked Keta.

"We're going to set an ambush along the river, back where it narrows. I am going to go ahead and meet the Seneca and ask for a parlay. I am going to try and talk to them."

Badger gasped. "You'll be killed!"

"Well, of course that's not part of the plan," said Tonti with a small, grim smile. "I need you and Keta to go along with the Indians to the island."

"I should stay here," said Badger. "There may be wounded."

Tonti hesitated. "No, I don't like that idea."

"I'll stay with her," said Keta.

"Who will go with the children, then?" asked Tonti.

"I will," said Stinky Henri. He took Alawa from Keta and held her in his arms like a small bundle. She blew her whistle happily in his ear. "I will see ze children safe to ze island."

Tonti nodded his approval.

"So that leaves me," said Robair. "Someone

needs to go after Segan."

"Yes," said Tonti. "You can go after him, but first I need someone to go with me to meet with the Seneca."

"Okay," said Robair. "Just as long as we are clear. After you and I take on those five hundred hostile Indians single handed, I need to go and take my musket away from the man who stole it."

"It's a deal," said Tonti and the two men shook hands.

"Hey, what about me?" I barked. "I've got more to do then chew on this old bone, you know, delicious as it is."

"What do you want to do, Pachelot?" asked Keta.

For an answer I took my bone and went to stand beside Tonti.

"All right then," said Robair. "Two men, a dog, and a soup bone against five hundred hostile Indians. It ought to be a good day."

After we made these plans everyone got very busy.

Archeveque turned up again and seemed to want to hang out with Stinky Henri. My theory is that Stinky Henri, smelling like all the meals he ever ate, was a comfort to Archeveque. In any case, old yellow eyes draped himself over Stinky Henri's shoulder like a mangy shawl and refused to leave. Stinky Henri seemed to like him there and even the Indian children seemed to want him around.

There is no accounting for taste.

We saw off the Indian children, women, and elders later that afternoon. Loaded with bundles that they carried on their backs, it was a slow procession that made its way out of the village and into the hills. Going across land would take less time, but it would still be slow with small children like Alawa to watch out for. Henri and some of the younger women carried five lightweight birch bark canoes with them. When they got to the shores of the lake, they would need some way to get across to the island.

The desertion of the Indian village left an eerie feeling in the air. As dusk settled in over the fort Tonti met with Robair and a group of men to discuss their plans again and make sure everything was in order for the ambush.

"Do you think this is going to work?" Badger asked Keta. We were sitting in front of a nice, warm fire. Badger was combing out my coat and the tangles in my tail. Unlike others I could mention, I do not enjoy looking scruffy.

"I don't know," said Keta frowning. "It is a very dangerous plan Tonti has decided to undertake. Do you think you have enough medicines to use?"

"It wouldn't hurt to gather some more," said Badger.

"Tomorrow, then," said Keta, "as we head for the new fort, I will keep an eye out."

Early in the morning I said good-bye to Badger and Keta. Badger wrapped her arms around my neck and buried her face in my fur. She held on for a very long time. Keta looked deep into my eyes and ruffled my ears.

"We'll see you at the new fort," he said.

I barked my agreement.

"Be careful," he said, and then they were gone.

I rode with Robair in his canoe as Tonti and the rest set out for the place of ambush. We reached it about dusk. The men moved as quietly as ghosts, hiding their canoes and hiding themselves. Along either side of the river the bank rose to small precipices of only about five or six feet above the water. The high ground ran for maybe a half mile before it descended into cedar swamp once more. Hidden on the high banks, the men intended to fire into the fleet of hostile Indians as their canoes passed under the overhangs. They would not be able to stop the attack or to kill all the attackers, but they would be able to diminish the numbers and delay the war party allowing the rest of Fort Crevecoeur the time they would need to retreat to the rock fortress.

They hoped.

The new fortress was a giant flat rock high above the river. It would allow a few men to defend it as long, as their food and ammunition could hold out.

The men, there were about a dozen of them, carrying pouches of food and water settled into their ambush positions. Tonti checked to make sure all was ready and then got in Robair's canoe. The three of us continued up the river as the darkness of night hid the world.

Overhead the stars, like chunks of crystal ice, shimmered in the blackness of the sky. Silently Robair and Tonti paddled, dipping into the dark water and pushing us forward with each stroke.

Dawn found us waiting on the riverbank in the spot Robair had recommended for Tonti's bold plan. As light began to illuminate the world, Tonti and Robair got busy cutting pine poles that they stuck into the soft muddy ground at the edge of the river. Tied to each of the poles was a white piece of cloth. A sharp breeze came up midmorning and the white pieces of cloth flapped and fluttered in a ghostly dance on the end of each pole.

From the canoe, Tonti took out a calumet carefully wrapped in ceremonial cloth. This peace pipe, he hoped, would convince the leaders of the war party to stop and honorably discuss terms.

Robair hauled his canoe deep into the woods and created a Badger disguise. I have to admit, I was very impressed. Badger's canoe hut had been very cleverly hidden in the woods near the Amikwa village, but when Robair finished with this one, the only way I could tell that it was there was by smelling it.

"It has to be good," Robair said to me. "We may need it."

Later, when he showed it to Tonti, or tried

to because Robair couldn't actually find it and I had to scout it out through smell, Tonti was also impressed.

"Let's just hope that nothing happens to Pachelot's nose in case we need to get here in a hurry," he said.

Then we returned to the riverbank and waited.

Late in the afternoon the wind began to pick up and dark clouds cloaked the sky. The air was chilly and thunder rumbled in the distance. The leaves from the trees whipped around us and floated in the water with a whispery whoosh.

And the first canoes of the hostile Indians appeared on the river.

XVII

The Attack

Tonti stood out on the bank so the Indians would be sure to see him. He held the calumet in his hands. Beside him Robair waved a smaller stick, which also bore a white cloth on its end. I stood beside Robair and tried to keep my fur from rising. The smell of hostile Indians was sharp in the air.

The river was a band of gray, the water choppy in the hard, cold wind. The Indians in the canoes were silent as they paddled strongly toward us, their painted bodies tense with effort.

When the Indians in the front canoes spied us, they immediately ceased paddling and the Indians in the center of the canoes put down their paddles and took up bows and arrows.

Tonti held out the pipe and Robair waved the flag like he was in a parade.

"We wish to talk in peace!" Tonti shouted out to them.

One of the canoes back paddled and turned around to meet up with another further behind. They were probably consulting the leaders of the war party.

At last one canoe filled with warriors made its way toward the bank. Tonti and Robair waited calmly as the canoe landed and six warriors, carrying war clubs decorated with scalps, tomahawks, and bows nocked with deadly arrows, approached.

"Easy, now, Pachelot," said Tonti softly. But really I think he was just talking to himself. I am always brave in the face of extreme danger.

The Indians approached.

"I am Henri de Tonti," said Tonti. "Commander of Fort Crevecoeur. We have had word of your war party."

The Indians exchanged looks. One Indian, his head shaved except for the brush of hair in the center of it, stepped forward. His face was painted a collision of reds and orange. His dark, angry eyes glinted in the gloomy light.

"Our warriors intend to destroy our enemy at Crevecoeur and kill any French vermin that try to stop us."

"Please," said Tonti calmly. "Let us sit down and smoke the pipe of peace and then we can talk."

With an angry gesture the Indian motioned for one of his fellows to come forward. This Indian, dressed and painted much like the other, stepped forward. In his hands he held a wampum belt.

"Black beads," muttered Robair.

Tonti nodded. Black beads were the signal for war.

The first Indian took the wampum belt and threw it on the ground at Tonti's feet. "The time for talking is over," he said.

And even before we knew what had happened, one of the Indians let fly with his arrow. The deadly iron-tipped weapon sliced the air and viciously buried itself in Tonti's side.

With a sharp cry of pain, Tonti staggered, dropped the peace pipe, and fell to the ground.

Immediately the Indians sent up an ear piercing whoop that was answered by the wild yells of their fellows in the canoes. Shaved Head leaped forward with his tomahawk raised to scalp the fallen Tonti, but found himself tussling with me instead.

Growling like every kind of demon I had ever heard of, I launched myself at the attacking enemy. My teeth clamped onto his arm and the weight of my flying fury toppled him backward.

Robair brought out a musket and fired into the rest of the attacking warriors as he yelled at Tonti to get up and get behind him.

The Indians in the canoes began to paddle toward us.

Tonti staggered to his feet and Robair got an arm under his shoulder. They ran, stumbling and staggering, for the cover of the woods.

I mauled the Indian under me and then launched myself at two others who tried to take off after Robair and Tonti. I heard the whistle of a tomahawk and twisted out of the way just as the blade thudded into the ground next to me. Barking and growling I ran in and out among the four still standing Indians, biting heels and nipping at the backs of legs.

The Indians danced around me and yelled furiously, but I would not let any of them past to chase Tonti and Robair.

And then two more canoes of Indians landed and began racing toward us.

Letting go of the arm of the Indian I had just crunched, I crouched in the face of the advancing enemy, every tooth bared and a growl to rival the thunder overhead rumbling in my throat.

The Indians yelled and a rain of arrows poured down on me. But I wasn't where they landed. I'm not stupid.

By the time the enemy realized this, I had disappeared into the woods, quick on the trail of Robair and Tonti.

I quickly caught up with the two men as they stumbled in the woods. They were going in the wrong direction. We could hear the hostile Indians tearing into the woods behind us.

"This way!" I barked.

Moving as quickly as we could we wove and rushed through the undergrowth reaching the hidden canoe before any of the Indians following had us in sight.

Quickly we rolled in under cover and seconds later the yelling and war whooping hoard of hostile

Indians were pelting by us. The woods were filled with them.

And then, suddenly, it began to rain. The sky opened up and thick, heavy, cold rain pelted down. Thunder crashed and the rain was a loud roar on the roof of our hiding place.

We waited, trying to calm our ragged breathing. Tonti's injury appeared serious. He held the white cloth from Robair's flag tight against his side. It was no longer white.

We waited.

The downpour only lasted several minutes. Soon it began to let up. We could no longer hear the wild whooping and yells of the hostile Indians. Tonti gasped a little in pain, bit his lip, and squeezed his eyes tightly shut.

We waited.

Soon the rain was only the occasional drip on the roof of our hiding place.

"Pachelot," said Robair softly. "Take a look."

I carefully began to squirm my way out of the hiding place, but before I got out, Robair stopped me. "Wait," he said. "You can't wear that. Someone might see you." Moving carefully so not to joggle Tonti, Robair removed my scarlet scarf. He was right, of course. Still, I didn't like to be without it.

The woods were wet and silent. Dusk was falling along with the drops of water from the now bare tree branches. Autumn was giving up the last of her colors.

I sniffed the air. I could smell hostile Indian, but it was the scent left as they had rampaged through.

I listened.

Silence.

Quietly, I made my way back to the beach. The poles had been torn down and broken. The peace pipe lay broken and half buried in the mud. I walked to the edge of the water. The ground was churned up and battered.

The river was empty. Nothing moved on its

flat gray surface.

The war party was gone.

I quickly made my way back to the hidden canoe. When I got there I barked the all clear. Even Robair understood the significance of me barking in the quiet woods.

He crawled out and then helped Tonti free. Tonti lay on the ground, his eyes closed. His face was the color of clay.

"He's hurt, Pachelot," said Robair. "An arrow in his side. The bleeding has stopped. I took the arrow out. He'll be okay, but we need to get him back to the others."

"I understand," I barked.

Robair, skinny as he was, was as strong as a bear. He carefully hoisted Tonti onto his back and gently carried him to the river. Then, while I stayed with Tonti, he went back for the canoe. We had undisguised it so he was able to find it by himself.

By the time Robair had settled Tonti in the

canoe, darkness had found us.

"Okay, Pachelot," he said. "Sit in that bow and stay alert. Somewhere ahead of us that ambush is being sprung. We don't want to run into any surprises."

Robair pushed us out into the river. I stuck my face well into the night breeze, still cold and fresh with rain, and stayed alert for the danger ahead.

XVIII

Segan

Ever the master in the canoe, Robair paddled us silently, smoothly ahead. We stayed on the river for about two hours, and then Robair decided it would be safer to wait until light before continuing.

When we came to a section of the river thick with reeds, Robair let the canoe skim easily into the dry rustling cover of it. In the dark we would be invisible to anyone who might be looking.

He gave Tonti some water, covered him with

some blankets and furs he had packed in the canoe, and made him as comfortable as he could. Then he, himself, settled down, stretching his long legs almost the length of the entire canoe.

But he didn't sleep. I know because he didn't snore, and the only time Robair didn't snore was when he was awake.

We waited out the night. I kept my nose on the edge of the canoe pointed to the river, but nothing came to alert me.

It was a cold night. My fur was fairly thick by then, getting ready for winter, but I pressed close to Tonti, in any case, sharing his warmth.

In the early hours of dawn two deer delicately stepped down to the river's edge for a morning drink. Robair watched them through the screen of reeds with a sort of goofy grin on his face. It was the same expression he had when he pet the alligator cat. The deer broke the thin skiff of ice with their sharp feet and dipped their noses to the cold water. When they finished they melted back into the woods like mist before the rays of the sun.

Robair waited for full light before we continued.

It took us another three hours to approach the ambush sight. As we came into the part of the river guarded by the precipices, Robair made the signal whistle. No one answered.

Hopefully, none of our men had been hurt, but the orders were that they were to go as quickly as possible ahead to rejoin the others in the new fortress. No one was to wait for us. Apparently, no one had.

We skimmed along through that stretch of water in eerie silence. We spotted three empty and broken canoes. There were no bodies.

We continued on.

About three miles further along the river, Robair again pulled the canoe to the bank.

He roused Tonti who had been resting fitfully. "It's too dangerous to continue along the river," he said. "I'll have to leave you here and go ahead for help."

"No," said Tonti his voice barely a whisper. "Send Pachelot. Go faster. Won't be seen."

"That's right!" I barked. "I can do it!"

"I suppose that's right," said Robair. "Okay. Only hurry, Pachelot, hurry!"

"I will!" I barked and plunged into the woods.

I could move fast now that I did not have to wait for humans and I made very good time. Running most of the time I made it to the fort ahead of the attacking force of Indians.

There I discovered the ambush men gathering and beginning their march to the new fortress. I ran to them barking and dancing impatiently.

They didn't recognize me.

Robair had taken off my scarlet scarf and none of these men knew me. They thought I was an Indian village dog. I am much more handsome than a village dog, of course, but these men had just fought a hard ambush and they were eager to get to their new defense. So they yelled at me, and threw an old moccasin that smelled like Stinky Henri at me, and I realized that none of them were going to listen to me.

I had to find Keta or Badger.

So I took off again and raced in the direction of the new fortress.

And that's how I found Segan.

It was an accident, really. I was tracing the path made by the others and I came across his scent when it crossed theirs. I paused to think about it for a minute and that's when I heard the gunshot. It was close by.

In any case, guns meant men, and maybe someone who would understand me. So I turned in the direction of the gunshot.

I found Segan when I came out of the woods along the river and discovered the edge of a long meadow of tall grasses. If I hadn't come out on a small hill, I never would have spotted him. As it was, I had to do some fancy spy hopping to see over the tall grasses that crested the hill.

Segan was out a little ways onto the meadow. He had shot a deer.

There was nothing I could do about it now. I had to find Keta or Badger so Segan was going to have to wait.

In the end, I had to race all the way to the new fortress before I could find anyone to help me. It was Badger I found at last. When she understood the need, she commandeered two soldiers to help carry Tonti on a pallet and, with Keta, we immediately started back to where I had left Robair and Tonti.

We traveled until it was too dark to see and then had to wait until morning. When we made our way back past Fort Crevecoeur, we had to make a wide detour. The war party had arrived and finding the village and fort abandoned, they had taken revenge by burning everything. Black smoke roiled into the air from the burning buildings and the burning fields.

"The fools," said one of the soldiers. "They're burning the food they will need for a siege."

"Fortunately for us," his companion answered.

We finally reached Robair and Tonti around midday. Tonti was okay, awake, and talking, but in pain. Badger quickly set to work on him.

I gave my news to Robair. And by that I mean that Keta actually told him while I danced about impatiently from one foot to the other barking the details and waving my tail.

"I've got to go after him," said Robair.

"Go," said Keta. "We can handle this."

"Pachelot," said Robair. "I need you. Will you come with me?"

"Of course!" I barked enthusiastically.

"He said yes, didn't he?" Robair grinned at Keta.

Robair decided to travel by canoe. Now that we knew where the war party was, it wouldn't be difficult to avoid them and it would be faster to travel that way.

So we set out. I guided Robair to the hill overlooking the meadow where I had last seen Segan. We found the remains of the deer he had killed, now a feast for birds and flies. Robair picked up his trail. Segan had returned to the river. He was on foot so Robair cached his canoe and we tracked along the banks on foot as well.

In the late afternoon we came to a place where the river branched. Segan had left the main river and followed the smaller branch. We followed this branch until it ended on the shores of a small wooded lake. In the middle of the lake there was an island.

"Pachelot," said Robair. "Do you know where we are? This is the island where the Illini children and women are hiding. Do you think Segan knows they are there?"

Cautiously, we followed his trail as it skirted the shoreline. Blue jays shrilled cries at us as we silently moved beneath the bare trees. And then suddenly, Segan's scent was gone. I followed it to the shoreline and then it disappeared.

I put my nose to the ground and zigzagged about hoping to find the scent again. Instead I found the whistle. It was half buried in the dirt by the lakeshore. It was one of the whistles Stinky Henri had carved for the children and beside it, clearly marked in the soft ground, was Segan's footprint.

Robair looked out toward the island, peaceful in the middle of the lake, a worried frown on his face.

"He knows they are there," he said softly.

XIX

Smallpox

"Pachelot," said Robair urgently. "We have to get out to that island!"

"We'll have to swim!" I barked.

"There's only one way to do that," said Robair. "We'll have to swim!"

"That's what I said," I growled as we waded out.

The lake bottom was mucky. I quickly pulled my paws off the bottom and began to swim. Robair floundered along for several more feet until he lost both moccasins to the sucking mud. After that, he simply dove in and swam.

It was not a very big lake, but it took Robair a certain amount of time to make it to the island. I had been ashore for quite a while, enough to be almost completely dry, by the time he staggered ashore.

I had waited to make sure he wasn't going to drown. You never knew with Robair.

Together we plunged into the wooded interior of the island. My nose was on full alert, but I knew that by the noise we were making everyone would know that we were coming.

Including Segan, wherever he was.

As it happened, we didn't find the Indians, they found us.

Robair had managed to get tangled in a blackberry briar patch and was not silently complaining about it when, all of a sudden, I looked up to see Alawa pointing a pudgy finger at him and screaming her little laugh. Her mother, a tall young woman with dark eyes and the same dimples as her daughter, was not far behind. Huyana was her name, and she thought Robair was funny too.

Robair turned several different shades of red. He did not like pretty girls to laugh at him, even if one was very small.

Huyana helped Robair untangle himself and then Alawa and her mother led us to the place on the island where the group had hidden themselves. All in all there were about thirty people. They had made some hide wigwams to rest in and kept small hidden fires for cooking food. They had spent the last several days trying to keep the children quiet and getting used to hiding. A tall white pine rose from the center of their camp. High in its branches, almost higher than I could see, Stinky Henri perched like a giant crow. He was the lookout.

Robair asked Huyana if anyone had seen Segan.

"No," she shook her head. "We have been keeping a careful look out. We have not seen anyone."

"You didn't see us either, though," Robair reminded her.

"Oh, that's true," she said the dimples appearing. "We had to hear you!"

Everyone laughed.

Robair scowled.

Stinky Henri climbed down from—or actually sort of fell out of—his tree to talk to Robair. He wanted to know how the attack was going and when they would all be able to leave the island.

"I don't know," said Robair. "But you must all stay hidden. The danger is not over. Come on, Pachelot. We need to explore this island."

"Perhaps I may help?" Huyana asked.

"No thank you," said Robair a bit gruffly. "We will be fine."

"I just thought you might need these," Huyana said, holding up a pair of new moccasins.

Robair's face did that strange coloring thing again. He accepted the moccasins. Then we set out.

Walking quieter this time we began a systematic exploration of the island. It was a small island. We found a little fresh water creek that rippled through the thickly wooded interior. There was evidence of beaver, especially along the shore on the far side. The beaver were not on the island, but I suspected that their lodges could not be far away. I could not smell any big animals, but there were rabbits and squirrels and grouse. We found more blackberry brambles. The trees were mostly pine and cedar and the ground swampy and low.

Sometimes I could smell Segan, but we couldn't find him.

One thing we knew for sure, invisible though he seemed to be, he was here. Somewhere.

When we got back to the clearing, Robair talked to Stinky Henri and Huyana. He did not want to alarm anyone, but they had to be warned about Segan and the weapon he carried.

"Where did you hide the canoes?"

Robair asked.

"There are down by ze little stream," said Stinky Henri.

"We hid them well," said Huyana.

"Still," said Robair. "We better check them."

Huyana guided us to where the five small birch bark canoes had been hidden. They were not far from the camp. They were well concealed, but they were within easy range in case they were needed for escape. Not that thirty some people could escape in five small canoes.

As night fell, the Indians put the children to bed. There were no lights, no fires. Only the stars, and later the moon, illuminated the wooded island.

As the camp became quiet, Robair settled himself at the foot of the white pine. Huyana gave him a blanket, but I knew that he intended to stay awake. I settled down beside him.

And he tried to stay awake, but he couldn't

quite do it. Soon a gentle snoring filled the quiet night. I sighed and rested my head on my paws. It would be up to me, I thought.

Along about moonrise, I was alerted to a stealthy rustle in the undergrowth. I raised my head and pointed my nose in the direction of the noise, trying to get a scent. I was all ready to raise the alarm when a porcupine shadowy shaped thing emerged from the edge of the trees.

Only it was not brother porcupine. The creature padded softly over and sat down only mere feet from my nose.

"Just when I think I've gotten rid of you for good, here you turn up again," said the shadow in a rough voice.

Archeveque.

"I feel much the same way," I growled.

"Just checking," said the cat. "I've been on the prowl since sundown. There is something not right on the island."

"Maybe it's you," I suggested.

"Something that wasn't here before, bone brain," he said. "I didn't find anything but I know that you are laying here pretending to be on guard."

"I am on guard!" I growled angrily.

"Only about as much as that snoring beanpole next to you."

Okay, so he had a point about the snoring, but as far as the alertness of my guard duty went, he did not know what he was talking about.

Archeveque thoughtfully licked the tip of one of his paws. "Anyway, I just thought you should know about it."

Then he got up and waving his tail in my face, he disappeared into the shadows.

Well, Archeveque might be the king of annoyances, but I knew that he was right. There was something wrong on the island and it was something that was extremely dangerous. I rested my chin on my paws, but I stayed alert.

And I did stay alert so I never will know how he did it.

As the graying light of dawn filtered in through the branches of the white pine I stood up and stretched. Robair had fallen over to the ground, completely asleep and was snoring loudly.

I stepped out from under the tree and then stopped dead in my tracks because there it was.

The iron box.

There it was, sitting innocently in the clearing amidst the little hide wigwams. And, what was worse, there was Alawa sitting in the dirt beside it. In one fist she held her little whistle. Her other hand was resting on the lid of the iron box.

A closed box, but a box that was no longer held shut by a lock.

Alawa giggled and began to open it.

"NO!" I barked and launched myself directly at the child.

I landed on her with my full weight and knocked her back, hard, to the ground. She was crying. I stood over her licking her face trying to comfort her, to get her to stop crying, when something hit me—viciously—in my side.

I gave a sharp yip of pain as the strike hurtled me away from Alawa, bowling me over in the dirt. I quickly regained my balance and turned with all teeth bared to confront my attacker.

He was ready for me.

It was Stinky Henri and he had a large and very knobby tree branch. He moved in yelling and swinging.

"Stop it!" It was Robair.

He wrestled the branch away from Stinky Henri, but he had to knock him down to get him to let go.

"Ze devil dog was trying to eat ze child!" yelled Stinky Henri.

By now everyone was awake. The clearing was filled with women wielding clubs and sticks and children, mostly boys, ready with stones to throw. Huyana ran forward and scooped up Alawa hugging her and comforting her.

"No, he wasn't!" Robair had to yell to make himself heard above the noise of crying children, screaming Stinky Henri, and shouting others.

"I saw him myself!" screeched Stinky Henri. "Give me ze branch! I will brain him, ze devil dog!"

"Stop it!" Robair shouted. He went over and scooped up the iron box. "Pachelot was saving Alawa from opening this!"

Instantly everyone was quiet. All eyes were riveted on the deadly box in Robair's hands.

And in the silence we all heard, very plainly, the sound of someone running away through the woods in a very big hurry.

XX

Robair's Musket

"Quickly, Pachelot! It's Segan!" Robair thrust the iron box into the hands of Stinky Henri who took it as though he had been given a live and very poisonous snake.

Then, with Stinky Henri's knotty pine branch and my iron teeth as our only weapons, Robair and I leaped into the woods in pursuit of Segan.

We could hear him crashing through the woods not far ahead.

"He's heading for the canoes," shouted

Robair. "Get him, Pachelot!"

That was all the encouragement I needed. I leaped ahead through the undergrowth, dodging fallen trees and briar patches, and I caught up to Segan as he was attempting to untangle one of the canoes from its hiding place.

With a growl I leaped on him.

Segan was a short and strong man. He yelled in surprise when I landed on him, but unlike Alawa who tumbled over like feather thistle, he didn't go down at all. He shouted and turned circles trying to shake me off. I had buried my teeth in the thick layers of his buckskin jacket and I did not intend to let go.

"I don't intend to let go," I growled through my clenched jaw.

"Stupid dog!" he shouted at me. "Let go of me!"

And then, somehow, he managed to grab me by the scruff of my neck and fling me off.

I landed in a tumble on the ground, but

turned to leap at him again.

And almost died.

Segan was there before me, taking dead aim at my head with Robair's stolen musket.

He fired.

For an instant I was both blinded and choked by the black gun smoke that swirled around me and deafened by the terrible roar of the gun as it fired.

But I wasn't dead.

The musket ball buried itself in the bole of a tree inches from my nose. Segan apparently did not know about the crooked shooting quality of Robair's musket.

And then Robair was there. He threw himself on Segan and the two went down in a tussle that carried them into the water. Barking like a mad dog I followed them as much as I could. They struggled and fought, the musket like a bar between them.

They were waist deep in the water. Fists flying and water spinning in the air, they pounded on each other. Soon the rest of the Indians, the women and elders and even some of the children, and Stinky Henri were gathered at the lake's edge. Sticks and clubs were at the ready to clobber Segan if he got within range.

But the final blow was Robair's. Wrestling his musket from Segan's grip at last, Robair flipped it around and crashed the heavy butt end of it down on Segan's unprotected head. Stunned, Segan swayed in the water before he gently collapsed into it, sending a small rippling wave to shore.

The Indians cheered and clapped their hands together as Robair dragged the unconscious Segan out of the water by the back of his shirt collar.

As they struggled to shore many hands reached out to help Robair haul in his burden. And then, suddenly, I saw something bob in the water and then sink in the shallows. Quickly I leaped from the shore's edge and swam out to where Robair's musket rested in the murky mud. I grabbed it like an old bone and dragged it to shore.

It had been broken at the breech.

Robair dragged Segan back to the camp area and the women tied him very tightly to the base of the white pine. He was still unconscious but was coming around.

Stinky Henri emerged from one of the wigwams carefully carrying the iron box. Everyone was silent, as though they were holding their breath. They watched as Stinky Henri handed the box over to Robair.

"I do not want zis thing anywhere near me!" he said. "What are we going to do with it?"

"I have an idea," said Robair.

First he begged an old beaver skin from one of the elder women in the tribe.

"Keta would approve of our use of this, wouldn't he, Pachelot?" said Robair as he carefully wrapped the skin around the iron box.

"Beaver are very strong medicine," Huyana agreed as she watched him. Robair made a bundle and trussed it tightly using his broken musket, as well as several stones, as weight.

"Come on, Pachelot," he called to me. "Let's get rid of this thing."

He and I got into one of the canoes and Robair gently paddled us to the middle of the lake at a spot that looked very deep. He tested it with a long pole he had brought along for this very purpose and found the spot to be over ten feet deep.

"Plus there will be a good foot or two of mucky mud at the bottom," he said cheerfully.

Robair dropped the bundle in and we watched it sink out of sight.

We waited on the island for three more days and then, at last, Stinky Henri gave the signal from the top of the white pine that some of Tonti's men had arrived. Keta was with them.

The attack was over. The Illini had returned from their pilgrimage and helped Tonti's men drive the remaining Seneca and Miami away.

"The Illini warriors came back just in time," said Keta. "We were running out of food and we were all getting hungry."

I thought about my soup bone. I hoped that it was still where I had buried it just outside the old fort, and I hoped I would be able to go back and get it.

"What happened to the fort?" I barked the question that was on my mind.

"Both the village and the fort have been burned," Keta said. "We won't be going back there."

Tragic.

"And the Illini will have to go somewhere else for the winter."

That wasn't exactly good news either.

The Illini thought they could find refuge with other tribes to the north but they wanted to get started before the real snows of winter set in. So we packed up the camp, including Segan and Archeveque ,who had again claimed Stinky Henri's shoulders as his personal territory, and marched all the way back to the new fortress, a place the

Indians had started calling Starved Rock.

There we rejoined Tonti and found Badger, who had stayed behind to help with people who had been injured. Segan was turned over to the soldiers. He would be carefully guarded and then would be taken to Quebec where he would have to stand trial and also answer some important questions. Questions like, who had given him the box of smallpox? So far he had refused to say anything at all.

So it was a cold morning some days later, with frosted trees and a skiff of ice on the lake, when Robair came looking for me. I had just returned from digging up my soup bone and I was feeling quite pleased with everything.

We walked down to the river together. Robair had his canoe pulled up on the bank but now he pushed it into the water, breaking apart the thin ice under its green trimmed prow.

"Well, Pachelot," he said, his hand holding

the stern of his boat to keep it from leaving without him.

This was Robair, remember. Anything could happen.

"This has been quite an adventure," he said. "I'm off to the north country now to try and stock up on some winter furs. I'll need to get me a good supply of them if I'm ever going to make myself rich."

"And buy yourself more tobacco!" I barked.

"That's right," he laughed. "Rich and famous."

I thumped my tail in agreement—after all, why not?

"You take care of yourself then, my friend. I'm glad you decided not to eat me, and I hope you like your bone!" For a man as long and bony as he was, he managed to get into his canoe with little difficulty even if, once or twice, it looked as though he might be going for an unplanned swim.

He pushed out into the deeper current of the

river. Doffing his muskrat cap to me he bent his back to his paddling and his canoe shot ahead like an arrow from a bow.

"Good-bye!" I danced a little from paw to paw as I barked my farewell. "Stay out of trouble! Good luck!"

My canoe is my home.

He began to sing in a loud, boisterous voice.

> *My hat keeps me warm.*
> *Pachelot is my friend*
> *He likes to chew bones!*

Soon he disappeared around the bend in the river and I could no longer hear his voice. I sat down on the bank and watched the morning sun lighten the depths of the water.

"There you are, Pachelot." It was Tonti. "I've been looking for you."

"I'm right here!" I barked.

"I have something for you," he said. Out of his back pocket he produced a new length of scarlet scarf. Stiffly, because his wound had not yet healed, he knelt and tied it around my neck. I licked his face.

"Tomorrow we'll get started ourselves," he said. "We should be able to catch up with La Salle in Quebec at the fur fair in the spring. I think he will be very glad to see you."

Together we started back to the high rock fortress above the river. Somewhere ahead of us I could hear Badger's flute and Keta's laughter.

"I am the Terror of the Woods!" I barked, lunging and prancing along in front of Tonti. "Better watch out for my iron teeth and my pirate's eye! I'm always ready for adventure!"

And with that, I ran up the trail to find my friends

The End

WENDY CASZATT-ALLEN is a teacher, poet, and playwright. She teaches 8th grade language arts in the Mid-Prairie Community School District in Iowa. A graduate of Interlochen in 1980, and of Michigan State in 1984, she went on to complete an Masters of Art at the University of Iowa, and is currently working on a Ph.D. in Language, Literacy, and Culture there as well. Recently her poetry has appeared in the Dunes Review. In addition, several of her plays for middle school players have been produced and performed on stage, as well as appearing on local television. She has given presentations at the Iowa Council of Teachers of English and Language Arts and at the National Council of Teachers of English on reading and writing with adolescents. She wrote *The Disappearance of Dinosaur Sue, Stolen Stegosaurus, Secret Sabertooth* and *Raptor's Revenge* with Michigan paleontologist PaleoJoe Kchodl.